Hey, TodaysGirls! Check out 2day's
kewlest music, books, and stuff
when u hit *spiritgirl.com*

Published in Nashville, Tennessee, by Tommy Nelson®, a division of Thomas Nelson,

Scripture quotations are from the *International Children's Bible®, New Century Ver*
Copyright © 1986, 1988, 1999 by Tommy Nelson®, a division of Thomas Nelson, In

"What If I Stumble" lyrics from DCTalk's Jesus Freak CD copyright © 1995 Pained
Music/Up In The Mix Music/Achtober Songs. Used with permission. All rights admir
tered by EMI Christian Music Publishing.

Creative director: Robin Crouch
Storyline development and series continuity: Dandi Daley Mackall
Computer programming consultant: Lucinda C. Thurman

Library of Congress Cataloging-in-Publication Data

Holl, Kristi
    4give&4get / written by Kristi Holl ; created by Terry Brown.
        p. cm. – (TodaysGirls.com ; 9)
    Summary: When fourteen-year-old Alex goes to Indiana to live with her grandparer
she struggles to cope with new friendships, her stern grandfather, and missing her
mother.
    ISBN 0-8499-7712-6
    [1. Family problems—Fiction. 2. Forgiveness—Fiction. 3. Grandparents—Fictio
4. Mothers and daughters—Fiction. 5. Christian life—Fiction. 6. Indiana—Fiction.
I. Title: Forgive & forget. II. Title: Forgive and forget. III. Brown, Terry, 1961– IV. S
PZ7.H7079 Aae 2001
[Fic]—dc21   2001030204

4GIVE & 4GET

WRITTEN BY
Kristi Holl

CREATED BY
Terry K. Brown

Thomas Nelson, Inc. • Nashville

Web Words

2 to/too

4 for

ACK! disgusted

AIMP always in my prayers

A/S/L age/sex/location

B4 before

BBL be back later

BBS be back soon

BD big deal

BF boyfriend

BFN bye for now

BRB be right back

BTW by the way

CU see you

Cuz because

CYAL8R see you later

Dunno don't know

Enuf enough

FWIW for what it's worth

FYI for your information

G2G or **GTG** I've got to go

GF girlfriend

GR8 great

H&K hug and kiss

IC I see

IN2 into

IRL in real life

JK just kidding

JLY Jesus loves you

JMO just my opinion

K okay

Kewl cool

KOTC kiss on the cheek

L8R later

LOL laugh out loud

LTNC long time no see

LY love you

NBD no big deal

NU new/knew

NW no way

OIC oh, I see

QT cutie

RO rock on

ROFL rolling on floor laughing

RU are you

SOL sooner or later

Splain explain

SWAK sealed with a kiss

SYS see you soon

Thanx (or) **thx** thanks

TNT till next time

TTFN ta ta for now

TTYL talk to you later

U you

U NO you know

UD you'd (you would)

UR your/you're/you are

WB welcome back

WBS write back soon

WTG way to go

Y why

(Note: Remember that capitalization may vary.)

iv

chapter.1

Chewing her thumbnail till it bled, Alex stared at her computer screen. She couldn't believe her eyes. Not again! Couldn't things go her way *just once?* Deep in thought, Alex mulled over her mom's e-mail message. Then, wiping her sweaty palms on her shirt, she hit *Reply* and typed,

That's great about your new job, but are you sure you can't come for Mother's Day? I've saved some money. I'll send it if you want.

Alex stroked the back of her purring cat, Maverick. Staring at the blinking cursor, she bit her lower lip, then leaned forward and added,

Please, please come.

Nodding then, she clicked *Send*.

She hated begging; it made her feel like a whiny baby. She shouldn't have to beg her own mother to come see her. This was the first Mother's Day in fourteen years they'd been apart, and today Texas seemed farther than the moon.

Alex clicked on the TodaysGirls.com icon and watched the magenta-and-silver screen load. One of the few good things about being exiled to Indiana was hooking up with some girls who had their own Web site and chat room. Granted, Amber was too goody-goody to be true, but Alex had learned from swimming with her on the relay team that she meant well. Just then a small window popped open with Amber's Thought for the Day. As usual, it annoyed Alex.

Hey girlfriends! Don't hold on to grudges, or grudges will hold on to you. Remember Matthew 6:12 says to forgive the sins we have done, just as we have forgiven those who did wrong to us.

Alex bristled. Easy for Amber to say. Alex bet nothing had ever happened in Amber's perfect little life to forgive! She closed the window then clicked on the chat room icon. Her screen name, TX2step, appeared in the otherwise empty chatter list. Where was everybody? Alex glanced over her shoulder at her bedside clock.

"Oh man," she muttered, shutting down her computer. She'd promised to meet her best friend, Morgan, at the Gnosh Pit fifteen minutes ago. Morgan's parents owned the restaurant, and tonight they were experimenting with something new to draw a bigger Friday night crowd.

Pulling an oversize shirt on over her tank top, Alex hitched up her baggy pants and clomped downstairs. Her grandparents sat in matching maroon recliners in the living room, watching a TV travelogue on Austria.

"I'm off," Alex said, making a beeline for the front door.

"Halt right there, young lady." Her grandfather twisted around in his chair. "Where do you think you're going?"

Alex clenched her jaw, took a deep breath, then turned around. She resented the third degree she got every time she stepped out the front door. Still, she bit her tongue. Smarting off would only get her another Friday night in the Old Folks Home. "I'm meeting Morgan at the Gnosh. I told her parents I'd be there for their first Karaoke Night."

"Their what?" He squinted as if that would help him hear better.

"*Care-ee-okey*," Alex said slowly.

"What's that?" he asked suspiciously.

Alex sighed. "People stand up and sing live to recorded music while following the words on a TV screen."

Grandpa frowned. "I don't want you singing rock music in public, do you understand?"

"No sweat." Alex brushed a chunk of frizzy hair back from her face. "I hate to sing, and I wouldn't be caught dead up front. I just want to support Morgan's family and help them have a good crowd."

"I bet that nice Amber from church will be there," Grandma said.

"That's right!" Alex flashed her grandmother a grateful look.

Grandpa pursed his lips into a prune while Alex studied the gray hair growing out his ears. "Be back by ten then. Not a minute later."

"Okay." *Cut me loose,* Alex thought as she hurried out the door and jumped on her bike.

Just minutes later, Alex locked her bike in a stand and headed for the Gnosh's front door. The blinds were still closed against the sun, but she could make out music. As she opened the door, the music reached a crescendo. An overflowing crowd filled the tables and spilled out of the booths. Alex glanced at the TodaysGirls booth by the window, amused to see Amber, Bren, Maya, and Morgan all googly eyed, staring toward the front of the room.

Music swelled again as Alex worked her way through the crowd. When she glanced at the singer, she did a double take. She knew he was an upperclassman. He was also one of the most gorgeous guys she'd ever seen. With blond hair sweeping low across his forehead, he sang words that took Alex's breath away. "'Take the keys here to my heart . . .'" The music softened, the young man closed his eyes, and his voice caressed each word. The buzz in Alex's ears kept her from hearing anything but snatches of the song's next verse.

When he returned to the chorus, his gaze moved across the crowd until it rested on Alex, nailing her to the spot. Alex was vaguely aware of people at nearby tables turning in her direction. Both embarrassed and flattered by the singer's attention, Alex felt her heart turn to mush as he finished the romantic ballad.

The music died, but whistles and shrieks filled the air. Blinking as she emerged from her trance, Alex felt heat creep up her neck as she slid into the booth with her friends.

"*Ooooh*, what was that all about?" Morgan squealed in Alex's ear.

"What was what?" Alex reached for Amber's leftover fries and a squeeze bottle of ketchup.

Order pad in hand, Jamie rushed over to their booth. "He was singing right *to* you, Alex! I didn't know you knew him!"

Alex shrugged. "You mean that guy up there?"

"Like yeah!" Morgan punched her arm just as Alex squeezed the ketchup bottle. A long red squirt splatted the front of her white shirt.

"Morgan!" Alex grabbed a paper napkin and scrubbed. The ketchup blob smeared from a small red streak to a medium orange blob. "Oh, crud," she muttered, dipping another napkin in Amber's water glass. She scrubbed her shirt again, managing to expand the medium orange blob into a *large* orange blob.

Bren arched an eyebrow. "You've been holding out on us, Alex! He's in some of my classes, and he's so cute! But how would he know you? Give!"

Alex turned her back on Bren. "So how's the Karaoke Night going?" she asked.

Morgan took her friend's cue and changed the subject. "It seems to be going pretty good. Most people are singing along."

"I messed around with the machine at home." Maya peered over her glasses. "You can even change the pitch of the songs so you can sing in your own range."

"Cool." Alex wished she had eyes in the back of her head. Where had that major hottie gone? More important, why had he singled *her* out like that?

Just then Morgan's friend Jared pushed to the microphone and bowed over his thick waist. "I'd like to perform for you 'Love Is Blue.'" He closed his eyes as the music played, but Alex couldn't help snickering. He was imitating the hottie, but the effect was a joke. Swaying back and forth with the mike, Jared wailed the lonely love song, something about a blue world and a gray life and black nights and green jealous hearts.

Amber grinned. "Hey, he's pretty good!"

Wild applause erupted when the music died, and Jared took three bows before handing over the mike. Alex surveyed the room quickly but saw no sign of the babe who'd sung to her.

Bren tapped Alex's arm with her French-tipped nails. "What are you not telling us?"

"What do you mean?" Alex asked.

"That good-looking junior just sang you a love song!" She fingered her double-pierced ear. "And hey, you're only fourteen. Leave the men to us older women!"

Alex felt her nostrils flare in what her dad called her "wild mustang" look. She didn't feel like pawing the ground, but she wouldn't have minded kicking Bren in the shins.

"Hey." Amber reached over and tapped Morgan's hand. "Your parents. They're not going to sing, are they?"

"Oh, no," Morgan said, twisting around. "They promised!"

"Puh-leez," sixteen-year-old Maya muttered, sliding down in the booth as if to hide. "They were supposed to stay hidden in the kitchen!"

Up front, Morgan and Maya's parents, the owners of the Gnosh, stood ready to sing, with arms around each other's waists. A lump formed in Alex's throat as she listened to them sing "I'll Be There." If only her *own* mother would sing that song . . .

Their voices blended amazingly well in the old Jackson Five hit as Mrs. Cross echoed her husband's words. It was all about reaching out and having faith in each other.

Alex bent over the cold fries and let her long curly hair fall across her face. If only her parents could love each other like that. Then all her problems would be over. Alex wondered if Morgan and Maya had any idea how lucky they were to have parents who loved each other and knew how to show it.

When the applause ended, Mrs. Cross called out, "We're turning it over to you young people now. Who's next?"

"Hey, how about us?" Amber jumped up, grabbed Maya's arm, then Bren's. "Let's show this place how TodaysGirls rock. We'll sing 'Lean on Me.'"

Bren smoothed her satin hair and designer shirt. "Look out, fans, here we come."

Maya grabbed her little sister's hand. "You guys come too."

Jamie untied her apron, dropped her order pad on the table, then joined them. Morgan slid out of the booth, her braces sparkling as she laughed, and pulled on Alex's arm.

"No way, Jose," Alex said. "I don't even know that song."

"You'll catch on. We sing it in youth group." Morgan kept pulling and wouldn't take no for an answer. The high school boys in the next booth noticed them and began to cheer. In defeat, Alex dragged herself up front but stood on the far end by Morgan.

It turned out that music for "Lean on Me" wasn't on the karaoke CD after all. "Oh well, we don't need music," Amber told Mr. Cross. "Enough people here know it." She grabbed the mike. "Everyone who knows 'Lean on Me' just sing along with us. Help us out." Amber hummed a few bars to find the pitch, nodded at Jamie and Maya, then started singing.

Feeling like a total fool, Alex tried to catch the words but found herself lip-syncing instead. *What* was she doing up there? She could have died. With no music, they sounded mega stupid!

Hiding her ketchup stain with one hand, Alex glanced around the room. Where was that . . . Oh, there he was, leaning against the glass counter by the cash register.

"'Lean on me . . . you're not . . . ,'" Alex mouthed, picking up a few words here and there. "'. . . need somebody to lean on . . .'" Self-consciously she pushed back her wild hair, wishing she'd combed it after her windy bike ride. She tried to see out of the corner of her eye. Sure enough, the blond hottie was staring right at her, a soft smile on his face.

As more people sang along, the volume rose. People at tables and those standing around the room synchronized their swaying. The TodaysGirls clapped and swayed, and despite her initial embarrassment, Alex felt the words pulse through her. "'. . . when you're not strong . . .'" She risked a glance at the boy and smiled uncertainly. "'. . . need somebody to lean on . . .'"

At the chorus, Alex leaned into Morgan's shoulder. Caught up in the admiration on the sea of faces, she opened up and sang with energy, right in Morgan's ear. Morgan jerked around, eyes wide. Alex grinned. Morgan obviously hadn't known Alex had such a strong voice.

At the end of the song, the crowd applauded. Mr. Cross gave each girl a high-five. "We should book you as an opening act every Friday," he said before disappearing through the swinging kitchen door.

Alex laughed at the idea and skirted around Morgan to head back to their booth. Suddenly she was face to face with the hottie. The blue-eyed hottie, Alex noted. He brushed back his blond hair and grinned. The blue-eyed hottie with dimples, Alex amended.

"Hey." He stepped closer and leaned down near Alex's ear so she could hear above the noisy crowd. "Just wanted to say I enjoyed your song. I'm Kevin Dean."

Alex crossed her arms over her stomach, hoping the ketchup stain was hidden. "Uh, nice to meet you." *Man, he smells good,* Alex thought. *What is that stuff he's wearing?*

"And your name is?"

"Uh, Alex. Like in Alexandra." Alex bit the inside of her cheek. What a dumb thing to say!

Kevin grinned. "Well, Alex-short-for-Alexandra, I was wondering if I could give you a call sometime."

Alex blinked and nodded. Out of the corner of her eye, she saw Maya and Bren staring from their booth.

"Could I have your phone number then?"

Alex choked. "My phone number?" Her mind produced several reasons why not. Mainly her grandparents. Alex pictured herself taking this babe's phone call in their living room, with Grandpa hovering nearby. "How about my e-mail instead? Are you online?" *Please say yes,* she begged silently.

"That's even better. Won't have to worry about calling too late and waking up your parents."

"Grandparents," Alex muttered. "I live with my grandparents." Alex moved with him to their booth, searching for something to write on. She reached for a white paper napkin. "Does anyone have a pen?"

"Why don't you write it for him in lipstick instead?" Bren suggested, reaching for her purse.

"Or better yet . . ." Maya glanced at Alex's shirt and held out the squeeze bottle. "Ketchup."

Bren laughed her tinkly laugh, and Alex wanted to drop through the floor.

chapter.2

Alex slipped Kevin her e-mail address, mortified that her hand shook.

He read what she wrote, then tucked the paper in his jeans pocket. "Well, itstexas4me, think we could go out sometime?"

"Uh, I don't know. I'll think about it. See ya." Eager to escape her friends' prying eyes, Alex pushed through the thinning crowd and headed for the rest room. She could hardly breathe, and the last thing she needed was to be grilled by Bren. Alex could hear someone singing karaoke while she scrubbed at the ketchup on her shirt. She couldn't believe what had just happened to her! By the time she'd listened to a second and third song, her breathing had returned to normal. She was reaching for the knob when a fist pounded on the door.

"You in there, Alex?" Morgan called.

Alex yanked the door open. "Can't a person even go to the bathroom?" She moved past her friend. "Sorry. Gotta go." Alex headed down the short hallway and past the kitchen.

"Wait!" Morgan caught up with her at the front door. "We can give you a ride home."

"I rode my bike."

"No problem. We'll throw it on the bike rack."

A minute later, Maya and Bren joined them. After anchoring Alex's bike to the rack, Alex and Morgan crawled in the back of Maya's old Volkswagen, Mr. Beep. Maya and Bren piled into the front seat.

Bren immediately turned around. "So spill your guts, Alex! We didn't know you knew Kevin."

"I never talked to him before tonight."

"Excuse me? I saw his eyes locked on you during his song!"

Maya raised an eyebrow at her in the rearview mirror. "Eye locks are one thing, but no lip locks."

"Ha-ha." Alex stared out the window, glad they couldn't see her flushed face. "Hey, can you take me home first? I'm expecting a call from my mom."

"Oh right." Bren sniffed. "I heard *him* ask for your phone number."

"I didn't give it to him!" Alex snapped.

"He wanted to call you, didn't he?" Morgan asked.

"Do you think he'll ask you out?" Maya glanced quickly over the backseat. "Listen, you're way too young. He's in my grade, not yours. Still, it would be fun getting you ready for a date. I could give you a makeover!" Maya practically bounced in the front seat. "I could update your clothes and maybe even tame that hair. You could be cute."

Alex fumed. Of all the nerve! "Look, you pinhead, my hair and clothes are plenty cool."

"I've seen you in public in *moccasins*," Maya corrected her. "I'm nervous that you'd wear them on a *date*."

"Who said I'd even consider a date? I only said hi to the guy."

"Stop it, you two," Morgan demanded.

"I'm only trying to help," Maya said. "And you can quit freaking out about Kevin. He's cool."

Morgan piped up. "Doesn't he go to your grandparents' church? Amber says he comes to youth group and really loves Christian music."

Oh great, Alex thought. *Not another one*. She really wasn't into this church thing at all.

Maya raised her voice over the car's chugging engine. "Kevin's in a band with Jacob's friend." Jacob was Morgan and Maya's older brother. "I heard they practice most nights in Kevin's garage."

A guy with a band? Alex perked up. Now that was more like it! Suddenly going to church didn't sound half bad, if *he* went there.

At home, Alex hurried to her room to check her e-mail on Grandma's ancient computer. Would she have heard back from her mom yet? Even more heartstopping, would she hear from Kevin?

As the computer beeped and squawked making the connection, Alex closed her eyes and let herself relive that awesome moment when Kevin caught her eye and sang right to her: "'You're always on my mind . . .'" As if riding over the top of a Ferris wheel, her stomach floated up, then dropped, and she felt dizzy.

Good grief, she thought. She'd read books where ditzy heroines' stomachs flip-flopped over gorgeous guys, but she'd thought it was totally not possible. She'd never admit it to a living soul, but now she knew it really happened.

When she clicked on her e-mail icon and typed her password, three messages loaded! Alex skimmed the Sender line and sighed. One was her Joke for the Day, one was a poem Grandma had sent to their neighborhood list serve, and one was from Morgan. "Tell me as soon as you hear from you-know-who!"

Alex wished she had something to tell! Closing down, she changed into her pajamas and scrubbed her face. Peering at her reflection, she wondered if she should let Maya try some makeup on her. She'd never worn any and swore she never would, but. . . . No, she decided, Kevin had liked her enough with no makeup to ask for her number. Anyway, she wasn't turning herself inside out for any guy. Not even the most totally gorgeous male she'd ever clamped eyes on.

For half an hour she surfed the Web, reading her favorite Texas tourist sites, but it only made her more homesick. Then at eleven she rechecked her In box. Still empty. Disappointed, she crawled into bed. But as she relived those electric moments at the Gnosh, she finally drifted off with a smile on her face.

First thing the next morning, Alex logged on again but still no mail. Why hadn't her mom responded yet? And why hadn't Kevin written to her? He'd seemed really sincere. What if he was just leading her on? What if he collected phone numbers and e-mail addresses from *every* girl that caught his eye?

She clicked on the TodaysGirls.com bookmark and waited while the silver-and-magenta home page loaded. *Welcome to TodaysGirls.com* flashed on the screen, then Amber's Thought for the Day popped up.

Matthew 6:14 says if you forgive others for the things they do wrong, then your Father in heaven will also forgive you for the things you do wrong.

Fess up, we all mess up! Don't let unforgiveness keep you in chains.

Alex rolled her eyes, then closed the pop-up window. She did *not* need to be preached at on an empty stomach!

Clicking the chat room icon, she entered her password, then saw her name pop into the viewer box with Morgan, Maya, and Bren. It had taken her weeks to keep everybody's screen names straight, but now in the chat room, she actually thought of Maya as *nycbutterfly*, Morgan as *jellybean,* and Bren as *chicChick*. Morgan had been her best friend since moving from Texas, and they were the only freshmen in the group. Alex refreshed her screen to load the last part of their conversation. Just as she thought. They were talking about Karaoke Night at the Gnosh.

nycbutterfly: mom & pop were happy with turnout. Not much $$$ made tho.

jellybean: 2 much singing & not enuf eating

chicChick: who could eat w/Alex's hottie makin' eyes @ her?

TX2step: WARNING! don't start on me!

jellybean: ignore them. Bren's jealous cuz he's in her class & didn't ask 4 her number

TX2step: he just knows the hottest chix R from down south

nycbutterfly: U go girl! 8-)

jellybean: I think Kevin & Alex should look deep in each others eyes and sing a duet

TX2step: in UR dreams. i'm gone

Alex clicked *Exit*. The last thing she needed was to be tormented about a guy who'd probably never give her the time of day again. Halfheartedly she clicked her private e-mail icon one last time. Her heart skipped a beat when a message loaded bearing the subject line: *RU there?* Alex grinned as she read:

Hello, Alex. I was glad to see you at the Gnosh last night. I've seen you around, but it was hard to talk to you since we don't have any classes together. You don't seem like all the other girls at school. I was hoping I could get to know you better. Say, could I come over tonight about seven? We could go for a drive or something. Let me know, okay? Kevin.

"Yes!" Alex bolted up from her chair and scared Maverick, who darted under the double bed. He liked her! Alex pushed her unruly hair back off her face and took two deep breaths. "Calm down," she whispered. "Think."

Flexing her fingers, she hit *Reply* and typed her answer, trying to sound as laid-back as he had.

I enjoyed meeting you too. Yes, I probably do stand out in the crowd, but who wants to look like the preppies

She stopped and frowned. Kevin might not like that. Backspacing, she erased half the line and began again.

but I'm from Texas, and styles are different there. Coming over tonight at 7 would be fine. I'm in Westbrook Village, which is on the west

**side of Main. Before I could go for a drive or
anything, you'll probably have to meet my grandparents when you come.**

Alex read and reread her message, checking spelling and
punctuation, then pressed *Send*. Stretching, she realized she was
sweating like a hog. She sniffed her armpit and about passed out.
If just answering Kevin's e-mail made her smell like a soured
dishcloth, she'd better roll on three layers of deodorant before he
came. In fact, she thought as she felt her stubbly bristles, she
might go all out and shave her legs.

She checked her e-mail several times, and an hour later,
Kevin sent a one-liner:

Glad it worked out--see you at 7.

Saturday passed in a daze until suddenly it was time to get ready.
Alex climbed into the claw-foot tub at six o'clock, wishing for
the millionth time her grandparents had a shower in their old
two-story house. She shaved carefully, and soon short black hairs
floated in soap scum on the water. She only nicked herself twice,
which was a miracle, considering how seldom she shaved.

In her bedroom Alex tried on a pair of capris, a Christmas
present from her mom that still had the tags on. Even with
smooth legs, Alex thought she looked stupid. Peeling them off,
she reached for a pair of bell-bottoms she'd once snatched from

a bag of clothes Maya was taking to Goodwill. Alex could zip them—barely—but the bell part dragged behind her a mile. Being five-foot-two could be such a pain.

She glanced at her bedside clock. 6:44! She flopped onto the bed, pulled off the bell-bottoms, and grabbed her favorite baggy pants with the side pockets. Over a blue-and-white-striped knit top she added a man's blue denim shirt. 6:50! In the bathroom she yanked a comb through her curly hair, then wetted it down to calm the frizzies. She peered into the mirror and groaned. A zit was definitely forming in the crease by her nose. Oh why didn't she own cover-up stuff like her friends?

Racing back down the hall, she glanced at the clock again: 6:57. Oh man. She jammed on her running shoes, but before she could tie them, she heard the doorbell ring. He was here! Alex clomped downstairs to the living room. "I'll get it," she called.

But Grandpa was already out of his chair. Alex hovered behind him as he opened the front door. She caught a glimpse of Kevin and heaved a sigh of relief. He was dressed in baggies and an oversize shirt too, plaid. She'd have died if she'd met him at the door in capri pants!

"Hello." Grandpa sounded puzzled.

"Is Alex here?"

"Yes. Come in, young man." Grandpa held the screen door as Kevin stepped inside. "I'm Alex's grandfather."

Alex smiled nervously and chewed her lower lip. Rats. She'd forgotten her lip gloss.

Kevin brushed back his long blond hair, then extended his hand. "I'm Kevin Dean."

"Kevin Dean what?"

"Just Dean. It's my last name."

"You're here to see Alex?"

"That's right. I thought we might go for a drive or something. If that's okay."

Grandpa glanced at the street. "That your car?"

"Yes. It's not fancy, but it's paid for!" He smiled at Grandpa, then Alex.

"And you're how old?"

"Seventeen. I'm a junior at Edgewood."

"You're too old for Alex, young man."

"Excuse me, sir?"

"I said you're too old."

Horrified, Alex wished she could drop through the floor. What was Grandpa doing? Trashing her first date before it started?

Grandpa took off his reading glasses and stuck them in his shirt pocket. "Don't take it personally, but Alex is too young to date." Grandpa opened the door and held it open.

"Grandpa!" Alex's hands were clenched at her sides. She couldn't risk looking at Kevin's face.

"I'm sorry," Kevin said quietly. "I shouldn't have come. I'll see you later, Alex." Without another word, he turned and walked past Grandpa and out the door.

chapter.3

"Grandpa!" Alex yelled. "What a rotten thing to—"

"Watch your tone of voice, young lady. I'm just looking out for you."

"I don't *want* you looking out for me! I'm doing fine on my own!"

"Your mother always said the same thing, but she was wrong too."

Just then Grandma came from the kitchen carrying a laundry basket. "What's the matter?"

"Grandpa just insulted the coolest guy from school, and he left. I never even got to talk to him."

"He was way too old for Alex. Remember what happened with Gail?" he added quietly, referring to Alex's mother.

Grandma nodded but was silent.

"I'm *not* my mother," Alex protested. "Grandpa was so rude to Kevin that he'll never speak to me again." Alex ran upstairs to her room and slammed the door so hard her window rattled. Maverick yowled and hid under the desk.

Alex collapsed on the bed and curled up in a ball, digging her fists into her eyes to keep from crying. She would *not* bawl like a baby just because that old goat had ruined the only decent thing to happen to her since she'd come to Edgewood. No wonder her own mom had run away at sixteen.

Maverick jumped lightly onto the bed, laid herself across Alex's stomach, and began to purr. Alex cradled the warm cat in the curve of her arm. Outside a moped whizzed by, then a car with a booming stereo. Ten minutes later Alex stretched to close the window. With the sun down, the air seemed to drop twenty degrees. She'd looked forward all day to this evening. What must Kevin think of her now?

Alex dragged herself to the computer and logged on to the Internet. Maybe her mom had answered her e-mail, but she refused to get her hopes up. What good did it ever do? Alex clicked on the e-mail icon and waited for two messages to load. One was an advertisement from a teen shopping site. The other Sender was listed as *kdean17*! She quickly opened his message.

Alex: I'm sorry things didn't go well tonight. I should have realized your grandparents would be old-fashioned and worry about my age. If

your grandpa ever gives me another chance, I'll
do better next time.

Alex's heart skipped a beat, then worked double time to catch
up. He wasn't mad! He'd said *next time!* She read on eagerly.

I honestly wasn't eavesdropping on you, but
after I left I couldn't help hearing you. Your front
windows were open. I'm sorry my coming over
caused trouble, but don't stay mad at your
grandfather, okay? Hope I see you at church
tomorrow. Kevin.

P.S. Do not be bitter or angry or mad. Never
shout angrily or say things to hurt others.
Ephesians 4:31.

Alex slumped back in her chair, the joy seeping out of her.
This sounded like a put-down now. Why did she have so many
religious fanatics in her life? Man, oh man. And yet. . . . She
twirled a strand of hair around her finger and pictured him
singing to her, then decided being a Christian was a minor flaw
in a guy so gorgeous . . . and so nice.

Clicking the *Print* button, Alex waited while her ancient printer
spit out a copy of Kevin's e-mail. She'd stash his letters somewhere
and read them whenever she wanted. Then she clicked *Reply.*

**Thank you for being so understanding about the
rotten way grandpa acted.**

She chewed her lower lip, debating how honest to be. After
all, she really liked this guy. It wouldn't cost her much to agree
with him, at least on screen.

**You're right about my yelling at him. I shouldn't
have. But that old coot is**

Oops. Alex stopped, then backspaced over her last sentence.

I hope I see you tomorrow too.

She reread her message four times, then pressed *Send.* Then
she found a used school folder in her desk drawer and slipped
Kevin's printed e-mail into it. She was ready to close down when
her e-mail icon blinked. She had more mail!

She opened it to find another message from Kevin! He must
have been online when she wrote. She leaned forward toward
the screen and read eagerly.

**I'm glad you're okay. I hope we see each other at
church too. It might be best if your grandpa didn't
see us together though! Ha! We'll just have to
e-mail for now. I'm a pretty good listener if you**

**ever need an ear. By the way, I think you're real
pretty. Kevin.**

Alex felt the heat rising up her neck to her face. Frizzy hair
and no makeup, and he thought she was pretty anyway! It blew
her away. She printed out his second note, then hit *Reply*.

**You're right about grandpa not seeing us talking at
church. Not yet. But I can tell you're a good listener.**

She told him about living her whole life in Texas until her
freshman year, then being sent to Edgewood when her parents
had some trouble. Hunched over the keyboard, she told him
about swimming freestyle on their school team and how much
she missed her mom. She moved the arrow over the *Send* button, held it there a moment, then clicked.

She stayed connected to the Internet while she went to wash
her face with Ivory soap and slather Vaseline on her lips. Her
stomach growled and she was tempted to go downstairs for a
snack, but decided against it. She'd just run into Grandpa and
want to rip his wrinkled head off.

Back in her room, she got into her pajamas, then checked the
computer one last time. She had *another* e-mail from Kevin!

**Thanks for telling me about yourself. You've
had a hard time of it, and I'm sorry for what**

your family's gone through. I've been luckier that way. My parents are solid--not perfect at all, but they love each other. I love music and play electric guitar. I was in marching band for a while, but then I quit when I decided to start my own band. Three guys from school practice with me most nights in my garage. Maybe you could listen to us practice sometime. Well, I'm glad we got to 'talk' tonight. Till tomorrow, Kevin.

Alex sat back in her chair, hugging herself. This had to be a dream! She printed out his third note, added it to the folder, then closed her e-mail. Splashed across the top of her browser's home page was a banner ad: "SEND AN ELECTRONIC MOTHER'S DAY CARD! When your mother lives across the miles, and you have to be apart, love grows even stronger when it's given from the heart."

Mother's Day. Alex sighed. She still hadn't heard from her mom. Was that card right? Did love grow stronger when your mom lived across the miles? Maya would probably agree. She always let boys dangle, waiting to hear from her, claiming that "absence made the heart grow fonder."

Alex leaned her chin on her fist. Was that rule true with moms too? Did they feel that way about their kids too? Or was it, as she was beginning to fear, "out of sight—out of mind"?

chapter.4

Sunday morning, Alex took more pains with her clothes than usual, actually ironing her plaid skirt. She caught a glimpse of Kevin when she arrived at church, but her grandfather ushered her briskly down the aisle to their front pew.

Alex didn't have the guts to turn around to see where Kevin was sitting. Afterward, she fumed as Grandpa stayed within two feet of her all the way out the door. Man alive! Nothing like having a sixty-five-year-old bodyguard.

She searched the halls for Kevin at school on Monday, but never spotted him. Being in different grades, they had no classes together, and he apparently had a different lunch period too. Her spirits sagged by the end of the day, but Alex rushed home in case he'd e-mailed her. Nothing. Not from Kevin or her mom either.

Downstairs, she'd just turned on the TV when someone

knocked on the door. Alex glanced out the porch window. "It's open!" she called.

"Hi." Morgan bounced into the room and rubbed her stomach. "I'm starving. Got any chocolate lying around?"

"I doubt it."

"Where's everybody?"

"At the grocery store. Grandma left a note. Come on."

Out in the kitchen, they spread peanut butter on Ritz crackers and built leaning towers of Cheez Whiz. Morgan chattered on about a cool Web site she'd found to help save endangered species. Humming the song Kevin had sung at Karaoke Night, Alex's mind wandered to more pleasant thoughts than South American lizards.

"What's that you're humming?" Morgan asked, interrupting her train of thought.

Alex blinked. "Don't you recognize it?"

"Uh. No." Morgan grinned. "You must have peanut butter stuck to your vocal cords."

Ten minutes later they were still eating when Alex's grandparents came in the back door. "Well, here are two of the famous songbirds!" Grandma said, peering over her grocery sack.

Alex cocked her head at Morgan, raised an eyebrow, then took the bag of groceries from her grandmother. "Wanna run that by us again?"

Grandma nodded at Morgan. "We bumped into your mother in frozen foods, and she told us!"

"Told you what?" Morgan asked.

"How you girls sang so beautifully at the restaurant. She said the crowd loved you and applauded and applauded."

Alex was warmed by the memory of Karaoke Night. "We *did* sound pretty good, didn't we?"

Morgan smiled but said nothing.

Grandpa carried in two more bags of groceries, then headed back outside. Grandma chatted as she put away the food. "I'm in charge of entertainment for the church's Mother's Day Banquet this year. I was racking my brains for ideas, and then voila! Mrs. Cross tells me about this natural talent right under my nose."

"Don't even go there," Alex warned.

"I don't think—" Morgan began. "Mom's biased. We weren't that good."

Grandma shook her finger at Morgan. "Now don't you get modest on me too. She said you sounded wonderful, and I won't take no for an answer. A row of beautiful daughters singing for their mothers? What better idea for a Mother's Day Banquet?"

"Dancing dogs would be a better idea," Alex said, grinning as she discovered the chocolate-marshmallow cookies in the sack. "Anyway, I thought Grandpa was against me singing in public."

"Oh, not at church! That's different. And you'd be all dressed up."

"You know, Alex, she's got a point." Morgan leaned against the counter. "Amber's mom would love it. So would Jamie's."

So would mine, if she ever came, Alex thought. She ripped open the box of cookies.

"Good. It's all settled." Grandma carefully folded the brown sacks and stashed them between the refrigerator and the wall, then bustled out of the kitchen. "I'll call everyone today."

As they ate the soft marshmallow cookies and drank cold milk, Morgan and Alex discussed the banquet. "I hate the idea of performing, even for Grandma," Alex said.

"Then maybe you shouldn't." Morgan took a gulp of milk. "I mean, since your own mom's not here."

"I did ask her to come for Mother's Day weekend, but she hasn't said yet." Alex crumpled the cookies' cellophane wrapper. "I really miss her. Do you think Mom misses Grandma?"

"Probably. My mom talks to my grandma a lot and sees her all the time, but she's just half an hour away."

"I wish . . ." Alex drained her glass and licked off her milk mustache. Surely she'd hear from her mom today.

That night at eight o'clock, Alex was first in the TodaysGirls.com chat room, eager for the nightly chat with her friends. Bren was in Kevin's grade. Alex hoped to find some way to ask about him without anyone *knowing* she was asking about him.

In rapid succession, the following lines appeared on her chat screen:

nycbutterfly is entering the room
jellybean is entering the room
chicChick is entering the room

rembrandt is entering the room

TX2step: it's about time. i've been here 4ever. <yawn>

jellybean: I can hardly move after eating four choco-marshmallow things

nycbutterfly: U 2 children will B tubbettes by June if U don't watch it

rembrandt: hey let's call our singing group the Tubbettes. what better place 4 tubbettes than @ a banquet?

chicChick: like yeah. Happy Mom's Day from your chubby children

faithful1: I don't think any1 can call us chubby. coach works us too hard!

TX2step: grandma talked 2 U already?

jellybean: I think she called every1 while we were chowing

rembrandt: my mom thinks it's a 1derful idea!

TX2step: my mom luvs it 2

jellybean: did U hear from her? is she coming?

TX2step: she'll be here M.D. weekend

chicChick: kewl. can't wait 2 meet her

Alex bit her lip. She wasn't *really* lying, just making an early announcement. Surely her mom would come for Mother's Day after she'd practically begged her. Any day now, maybe even later that night, her mom would say she was coming. No big deal if Alex told her friends a little early.

nycbutterfly: hey Alex she can meet your new BF when she comes

TX2step: he's not my boyfriend!

faithful1: but he is a hot, hot, hottie!

nycbutterfly: he could B if u played your cards right. I should take you shopping. A new U would knock him dead

TX2step: u 4get. No $$$$

chicChick: even w/new clothes he's still 2 old 4 u. he's robbing the cradle

nycbutterfly: Bren, B quiet. I know some good fashion sites 4 u to check out, Alex. lots of free advice there to fix you up. I'll send them 2 u

TX2step: don't bother

nycbutterfly: it's no bother. I want 2 do this 4 u. it'll be so much fun.

chicChick: even if there wasn't a guy involved, a new wardrobe is in order. fashion knowledge should be shared with those less fortunate

Alex nearly gagged. Did they actually believe she was *grateful* for their "help"? Talk about giant helium heads!

jellybean: I feel sick. i'm going 2 bed

nycbutterfly: that's what u get 4 a chocolate pig-out

jellybean: whatever. night all!
jellybean left the room

Alex watched a flurry of good-byes appear as the girls remembered chemistry quizzes, poetry papers, and algebraic agony. Alex checked her e-mail again. Nothing. Sighing, she surfed to her favorite search engine to *Ask Jeeves* about contemporary Christian music. The next time Kevin talked about it, she intended to wow him with her current knowledge.

For an hour she followed the links turned up by her search. At www.ccmusic.org she clicked on a link called Artists but recognized none of the names. She clicked on one possibility, the David Mainor Band, which loaded a page featuring four guys older than her dad. One was totally bald! A headline called them "a rock band with a mission: to reach out to the lost and backslidden."

Flabbergasted, Alex slumped back in her chair. Was *this* the kind of music Kevin was into? These geezers were old hippies, with long ponytails in back and no hair in front. Their profiles belonged on Get-A-Geezer.com.

She hit her *Back* button, then scrolled down farther. One group, Plus One, had a list of sub-links. *Must be popular guys,* Alex thought. She clicked and waited. As the photos loaded, Alex leaned close to the screen. Whoa! This wasn't half bad!

Photos at the Promo Tour Guide showed five hot guys on-stage, then some pictures of them just clowning around. There were "raw concert clips" that she could have downloaded if their dinosaur computer had more memory. These guys were definitely cool.

Not a geeky one in the bunch. Alex jotted down several song titles on their CD *The Promise* that caught her eye: "Written on My Heart," "I Run to You," and "I Will Rescue You."

A knock on her bedroom door startled her. "Alex honey?" Her grandma poked her gray head inside. "You about ready for bed?"

"Yeah, soon."

"Still chatting with your friends?"

"Doing some research."

"Well, try to wind it up soon. It's a school night."

"No problem." Alex jumped up and grabbed the door as it was closing. "Grandma?"

"What, honey?"

Alex jammed her hands in her pockets. "Do you think Mom will come for Mother's Day? Have you heard from her?"

"Not lately. It would be a special Mother's Day for *me,* too, if Gail came home. I miss my only daughter."

Alex hugged her grandma, patting her curved back. "I miss her too. Night, Grandma."

Back at the computer, Alex checked her e-mail. Still nothing. She chewed her thumbnail, wishing she didn't feel so stupid about the stuff Kevin was interested in. Well, she wasn't dumb. She could learn.

Snapping off her lamp so no light showed under her door,

Alex typed in a question about electric guitars at *Ask Jeeves*. She soon learned that there was a whole special language for guitars. Words like trapeze tailpiece, P-90 pickups, 22 fret fingerboards, humbucking pickups, and pearl block inlays filled the Web sites. She rubbed her tired eyes. They might as well be speaking Greek.

Still, she could drop a few of the phrases into her conversation and show Kevin she wasn't totally ignorant. Then he'd realize he could really talk to her. After that, all she'd need to do to keep him talking was nod and bat her eyes like Bren. Alex pursed her lips. Skip batting the eyes. She could never pull that off. What about gazing deeply into his eyes while he talked? Yeah, she could about handle that.

No time like the present to impress. Alex opened her e-mail account, clicked *New Message*, then wrote:

Hi, Kevin. I think it's neat that you like Christian rock music. I suppose you've heard of Plus One? They're cool, especially their album

Alex paused and studied her notes.

called THE PROMISE. I really like the song Written on My Heart. Oh, and I hope I can hear you practice sometime. Thanks for asking me. What kind of electric guitar do you have? I miss my

She peered at her notes again.

Gibson '67 Flying V Guitar. I left it back home in Texas. Well, off to bed. Talk soon. Alex

There, she thought, that should impress him. She'd show Bren and Maya she didn't need their lame fashion makeovers. Kevin already liked her, even though they were really different.

After closing her e-mail, she pressed the *Back* button, then returned to the Christian music site. She really wanted to understand Kevin's interest in this type of music. Curious, she clicked on the Teen Links button on the left side of the screen. There she found about fifty teen hangout sites. Cyberteen looked interesting, so she clicked there.

It had the usual neon colors, blinking graphics, and fashion advice, but a headline halfway down the page caught Alex's eye: "Crush-Worthy Quiz." Alex leaned closer to the screen and read. "Is your heartthrob really worthy of your time and attention? Take this quiz and find out!"

She was cautioned to "submit accurate information for best results." Alex grinned. This looked fun. At the end of the quiz, your results would be sent if you filled in the e-mail address line.

There were ten questions to answer, starting with the name of the guy Alex hoped was crush-worthy. *Kevin,* she carefully typed. Other questions asked her: *Do you like his friends? Do you believe he is honest? Do you know his favorite color? What is his favorite number? Does he prefer the ocean or the lake? Do you like his choice of movies?* Many choices were listed for each question. Alex gave each one careful thought.

After she hit *Click Here to Submit*, it suggested taking the test a second time, from the guy's point of view. Did he like her friends? Alex thought so. Did he know her favorite colors and movies? She had to guess. Grinning, she typed in his e-mail address and answers she thought Kevin might give. When she'd done her best, she pressed *Click Here to Submit*. When his test results were e-mailed to her, she'd compare their answers.

She bet they were a perfect match.

She clicked her e-mail icon and watched a message load with *Crush-Worthy Quiz!* in the subject line. She read the results silently.

Alex, you are deeply in love, or soon will be, with Kevin. He is a man of high ideals. He is a very alert person. He likes parties and is usually hyper.

Alex snickered. Kevin was never hyper.

He is a mellow person and likes to keep to himself.

Well, that was true, but how could he be both mellow and hyper? Even if it was sappy, she couldn't wait to read the results of Kevin's quiz and see if they were compatible. Where was it anyway? Alex waited, then clicked the e-mail icon again. His results should have been instantaneous too. Obviously the Web site had preprinted answers ready to send.

Then a horrifying thought struck Alex, and her mouth dropped open. On Kevin's quiz, she'd filled in *his* e-mail address. That stupid site had probably sent the results to *him*. Was that possible? Was he reading it at this very minute? She wanted to croak.

In vivid color, she imagined Kevin logging on and seeing *Crush-Worthy Quiz!* then reading "Kevin, you are deeply in love, or soon will be, with Alex!"

Alex could barely draw a breath. How could she have done something so lame? How could she ever look Kevin in the face again? What if he told his friends? What if he told *her* friends? This would be the living end.

Alex logged off and sat, frozen. Eventually her swimming fish screen saver appeared, then after a while the screen went black. Finally she stumbled across the dark room and into bed.

After a restless night, alternating between nightmares and staring at the dark ceiling, Alex turned off her alarm before it rang. She checked her e-mail again, hoping against hope that Kevin's quiz results had arrived during the night. No such luck. Nothing from the online love quiz, or from Kevin, or from her mom.

With dread in her heart, Alex dressed and tried to eat breakfast but couldn't. At school, she spotted him at his locker but ducked into the rest room to wait till he left. She didn't see Kevin all day but thought she glimpsed his blond head after school. She craned her neck. Was that Bren waiting with him at his locker? It was! Alex wanted to die when she saw them turn, laughing, and leave the building together. The tightness in her chest made it hard to breathe as she headed toward the bike rack.

At home her grandparents were outside planting flats of red and white impatiens in the flower beds at the side of the house. After carrying several buckets of water to them, Alex trudged inside. She grabbed a box of graham crackers on her way through the kitchen, then headed upstairs to check her e-mail. After it loaded, she took a quick breath. She had mail from Kevin!

The message was a forwarded attachment. Alex knew what it was even before reading his message. It began:

Alex: I think I got these quiz results by mistake.

Alex closed her eyes as the room began to spin.

chapter.5

Alex's hands shook. She closed her eyes, forced herself to take a deep breath, then began reading Kevin's e-mail.

Alex: I think I got these quiz results by mistake. Don't be embarrassed. Once I accidentally sent a message to my MOM instead of my brother at college, with some pretty private things in it. It happens to all of us eventually.

Alex gripped her hands together till her fingers ached. She couldn't believe how understanding he was.

Actually I'm kind of flattered, so don't beat yourself up. One line there claimed that someone

41

special had a crush on me. I wouldn't mind! Take
care. Kevin.

Alex's heart beat faster as she scrolled down to read the forwarded message. As she suspected, it started out the same:

*Kevin, you are deeply in love, or soon will be,
with Alex. You are a very alert person and your
life is full of love. Someone has a huge crush on
you. You have a good love life already, but it
will soon grow.*

Alex rubbed the back of her neck, then printed the e-mail
and stuck it in her folder. Biting the edge of her lip, Alex clicked
New Message and typed the address *kdean_17@hotmail.com*.

Kevin: I feel real silly about that dumb quiz.
Thanks for being so nice about it. I wanted to
hide when I figured out what happened.

She paused, lightly tapping her fingertips on the keyboard.
Since he'd been so understanding, did she dare? Why not?

The Crosses are having karaoke again at the
Gnosh Friday night. Think you might come?
Hope so.

And she pressed *Send.*

Alex checked her e-mail twice Monday night and again several times on Tuesday but no answer. Her hope slowly leaked away and was replaced by dread. Oh, why had she mentioned Friday night? Now he'd think she was chasing him or expecting him to sing her another love song!

She also wrote to her mom again, telling her that she was performing with her friends for the banquet. She hoped that would convince her mother to come. Alex had even called long-distance, but no one answered. She feared that the long silence meant something bad had happened at home again.

On Wednesday morning before school, Alex found one message in her In box. It was from Kevin. He'd ignored her question about Friday night but had written:

You have a Gibson 1967 Flying V Guitar back in Texas??!! Not to be nosy, but how could you afford it? They cost over $4,000! Would I love to see that!! Kevin.

Alex gulped. Four thousand dollars? How could that be? Alex frantically sorted through her research notes. She hadn't written down any prices, but she definitely remembered electric guitars for sale online for less than two hundred dollars! How had she picked one so expensive? It was *old*, for Pete's sake, practically junk. Of course, maybe it wasn't just old—maybe it was a classic, like a car.

"Me and my big mouth," she muttered, clicking the message box closed. What was she going to do *now*?

All day long Alex zoned out in her classes, trying to concoct a believable explanation. In English, she drafted five different notes, then crumpled each one. Even though her dad *had* actually owned an old guitar at one time—and Alex had experimented with the chords—it probably hadn't cost more than a hundred dollars. It had wound up in some pawnshop during one of her dad's layoffs.

After school, Alex reread Kevin's message and sighed. She might as well confess. Kevin had understood about the Crush-Worthy Quiz, so maybe he'd overlook this too. Alex swore that this was the last time she'd do something so stupid.

She clicked on *New Message*.

Kevin: This is so embarrassing. AGAIN. I wanted to impress you with my vast knowledge of electric guitars, but I really don't know squat about them. I learned about Gibson guitars on the Internet. My dad just had a cheap guitar a few years ago. Sorry. I feel like an idiot. I still hope you'll come Friday night. Alex.

She reread her message several times, then pressed *Send*. Then she sent one more message to her mom.

Dear Mom, Are you okay down there? You aren't answering my messages, and no one's there when I call. Please call or write. Please come for Mother's Day.

Alex wanted to add *Do you even remember you have a daughter?* but didn't. Somewhere under her worry a deep pool of anger and hurt simmered. Alex felt like she'd been shipped north and forgotten about.

Thursday and Friday dragged on forever, with no word from either her mother or Kevin. If she hadn't promised Morgan she'd come again, Alex would have skipped Karaoke Night. She didn't feel up to faking a good time. She arrived out of breath from her bike ride and slipped into the booth with Bren and Morgan. Mr. Cross was setting up the karaoke player against the back wall.

Amber hustled over with her order pad.

Alex raised one eyebrow. "How come you're working?"

Amber nodded toward a table in back. "Jamie had to babysit Coach's boys. She brought them with her tonight. Burger and Coke?" she asked, scribbling Alex's regular order.

"No, not tonight."

"Oh, come on." Bren slid the squeeze bottle of ketchup toward her. "Eat it or wear it."

"Ha-ha." Alex glanced at Amber. "Just the Coke."

"Testing, testing," Mr. Cross boomed into the microphone. "Who wants to kick off our second Karaoke Night with a song?"

No one volunteered.

"Come on, don't be shy." Mr. Cross meandered through the crowded room, then stopped at the girls' booth and grinned. "I think I've found our first act."

"No, Dad," Morgan pleaded. "We don't want to be first."

"If you don't come now, your mom and I will sing again."

"Anything but that!"

Mr. Cross pulled her to her feet. "You too," he said, reaching for Alex's hand.

"Don't make Alex sing." Morgan tugged on her dad's arm. "I'll go."

"Nonsense." He pulled Alex to her feet, too, but Bren shrank back into the booth's corner, out of reach.

On the way up front, Alex pulled Jamie's blonde ponytail, which stuck out from her baseball cap. "Come on," she said. "The more, the merrier!"

Nat Short jumped up. "We'll help, Jamie!"

Jamie paused. "No, you boys stay in your chairs. You can sing along from here."

Up front, Jamie stood on one side, Alex was in the middle, with Morgan on the other side.

Jamie read from the back of the CD cover. "This song is called 'You Can't Hurry Love,' and it's by Diana Ross and the Supremes."

Alex struck a casual pose, singing the words on the TV screen: "You can't hurry love, No, you just have to wait . . ." The words were new to her, but Alex loved the tune. Just as she leaned close to Morgan to sing into the mike, Christopher Short dashed up front, laughed, and grabbed the microphone from Morgan.

"Go back and sit down!" Jamie said, rolling her eyes at the girls in apology.

"Give us back the mike," Alex added.

"No!" Christopher thumped Alex's arm. "You stink! We sing better than you." The audience laughed, and his shrill voice made Alex wince. She could barely hear herself over his screeching.

"'. . . she said love don't come easy, It's a game of give and take.'" The lyrics brought Kevin to mind, how he'd sung to her last week. If only he were there again.

Just then the front door opened, and Kevin walked in. Bren waved wildly from the booth. With his eyes on Alex, Kevin worked through the crowd to sit with Bren.

Alex's stomach tied in knots as she continued to sing. Bren chatted with Kevin, touching his arm and rolling her eyes, lowering her lashes, then blinking rapidly. Alex wanted to hurl. Did Bren have to flirt with everything in pants? Alex barely moved her lips through the rest of the love song.

After thunderous applause, Jamie asked who wanted to sing next. Four or five hands shot in the air. Head down, Alex zigzagged through the crowd back to their booth.

As she came up behind them, Bren was recounting some story, waving her hands in the air, then touching Kevin's arm for emphasis. "Last week I had that flu bug myself. Oh, the agony!" Then she waved her fingers at Alex. "Well, here she is, Miss Karaoke Queen!" She leaned across the booth and actually *winked* at Kevin. "Say, did you get my e-mail? I sent you something hilarious!"

Alex itched to clobber Bren. Why was she e-mailing Kevin? And how did she get his address in the first place? Did every girl in school have it?

Morgan slipped around Alex and slid into the booth beside Bren. If Alex sat down now, she'd have to sit by Kevin or look silly by squeezing into the opposite seat with her two friends. Just then Amber arrived with her ordering pad and draped an arm over Alex's shoulders. "Hi, Kevin. Need anything from the kitchen?"

"Maybe later. Thanks."

"Sure. I'll check back." Amber stared hard at Alex, then pulled her aside. "Hey, can I talk to you for a minute?" she said.

"What's going on?"

"I saw you watching Bren while you were singing." Amber's eyes were warm with sympathy. "Don't take her personally. She's not flirting. That's just Bren. She's the same way with everybody, guys and girls both."

Not flirting? Alex thought. *Get real!* "It doesn't matter. It's not like he's my boyfriend or anything." Alex crossed her arms tightly over her chest.

"Just don't be mad, okay? Bren's harmless."

Alex's eyes narrowed at the sound of Bren's laughter. *Harmless like a black widow spider,* she thought. "No big deal," she said aloud. After Amber disappeared through the kitchen's swinging door, Alex returned to their booth, determined to plaster a smile on her face. No one, *especially* not Kevin, would know she was mad enough at Bren to spit nails.

Kevin stood up to let her in. "I'm glad I heard part of your song," he said, glancing from Morgan to Alex, "but I think I should have stayed in bed."

"I'm sorry you were sick," Alex said, afraid to look directly at him. What she really wanted to ask was *Did you get my e-mail? Are you angry about the guitar? Are we still friends?*

"I think I'm going to take off. See ya later." He nodded, gave a small wave, and left. Alex sighed and sipped her Coke as he disappeared, leaving her questions unanswered.

She slept fitfully that night, crawling out of bed after ten Saturday morning, more tired than when she'd gone to bed. She dreaded the dismal day ahead. After pulling on some baggy sweats, she checked her e-mail. Nothing. *Again.*

Grabbing her science project and lab notes, she trudged downstairs. Through the kitchen window she saw her grandparents planting their vegetable garden out back. Already several rows were marked off with stakes topped with seed packets.

Alex grabbed a can of Mountain Dew from the refrigerator

and drank it fast for the caffeine jolt. She spread out her papers and folders on the table. She'd rather clean Grandpa McGee's dentures with her own toothbrush than do homework! Once she graduated, she'd never set foot inside another school as long as she lived.

At ten-thirty Grandpa came inside. "Good morning."

"Morning." Alex surveyed the mess of lab notes on the kitchen table. "Actually, *good* is a real stretch."

"What are you writing?" he asked, peering over her shoulder.

Annoyed, Alex leaned over her report. She *hated* when people read over her shoulder. Shifting to hide her work, her arm brushed against a stack of folders. "Man!" she said, watching the papers scatter across the floor.

"I'll get them." Grandpa squatted, his knees cracking. He began to gather up papers.

Alex reached for her pencil where it had rolled under her chair, then straightened. Her grandfather frowned as he stared at one of her papers. *Oh crud,* Alex thought, *did he find that test I got a D on?* This just *wasn't* her day. "I can explain about that."

Grandpa stood, his joints popping again. "I doubt it."

"That stuff wasn't even covered in the book!" Alex protested.

"I'm sure it wasn't."

"It's true! Just read those questions."

Grandpa's voice was ominously quiet. "'You have a good love life already, but it will soon grow.'" His eyes snapped. "Just who is *kdean17,* or need I ask?"

Alex froze. He was reading the Crush-Worthy Quiz results Kevin had forwarded to her!

"Let me get this straight, Alexandra. I told him he was too old for you, so he goes behind my back and writes you love letters?" He tossed the e-mail down on the table.

"You don't understand," Alex spluttered. "He didn't."

"I understand more than you think." He sounded both angry and sad. "I've been through this before—with your mother!"

"If you didn't give her any privacy either, no wonder she ran away! I'm amazed she lasted sixteen years!" Alex scooped up her papers and books and stormed out of the kitchen and upstairs. In her room she threw herself crossways on the bed. What an old snoop! He had *no right* to read her personal stuff. If only she could talk to her mom about this.

Thinking of her mom, she rolled to a sitting position and waited for the throbbing in her temples to subside. Then she logged on to check her e-mail. Her mom's name popped up in the Sender column, and Alex sat forward so fast she cracked her knee on her desk. Quickly she opened her message.

Hi, Sweetie! I just got your earlier e-mail. The computer's down at home, and I don't have access to the Internet on my new job. I'm at the library right now using theirs. How are you? I know I just saw you six weeks ago on spring break, but it seems so long ago already. As much as I'd love to come up for Mother's Day, I can't ask for time off right after starting a new job. They'd never let me. Besides, I don't have the money for a ticket right now. But believe me, I will miss you on that day. Have Grandma take lots of pictures of you singing at the banquet. Then I'd feel like I was part of your day, at least in a small way. Be good, Alex, and get along with Grandpa. I know he can be trying at times. I love you. Don't ever forget that. XOXOXOXXOXOOXOX Love, Mom

Alex's shoulders slumped. Her mom wasn't coming. She hadn't even *asked* for time off. Alex would be the only girl at the Mother's Day banquet without a mother.

She closed her e-mail without replying. What difference would it make? Nobody listened to her anyway. Nobody cared how *she* felt.

Well, except Morgan. Maybe she was in the TodaysGirls.com chat room right now. Alex clicked the chat bookmark and waited while the magenta-and-silver screen slowly loaded. Although the chat room was empty, Amber's Thought for the Day popped open. Alex scowled as she read.

Remember that forgiveness works both ways. If we want forgiveness, we need to offer it to others. Matthew 6:15 says if you don't forgive the wrongs of others, then your Father in heaven will not forgive the wrong things you do.

How typically unfair of the whole Christian system, Alex thought in disgust. Her mom wouldn't even try to visit her in exile, and Grandpa ripped her head off after reading her private mail. Yet *she* was supposed to forgive them if she wanted God to forgive *her?* Talk about injustice! The stuff Alex did—like pretending to own an old guitar—wasn't nearly as bad as the junk that was done to her. Not even close.

chapter.6

That night about seven Alex was in her room and happened to glance out her window in time to see Grandpa drive away. Curious, she padded down to the kitchen. "Whatcha making?" she asked her grandmother.

Grandma turned a wad of dry-looking dough onto a lightly floured board. "Irish soda bread for tomorrow." She kneaded the dough for a minute, then shaped it into a round about eight inches across.

Alex reached in a cupboard for a handful of miniature marshmallows. "Where'd Grandpa go?"

"To help set up a puppet stage for children's church tomorrow." Grandma placed the circle of dough on a baking sheet, then cut a cross half an inch deep in the top.

"When will he be back?" Alex asked, pouring herself a glass of milk.

"A couple hours, I imagine." She wiped her face with the back of her hand, leaving a flour streak across her cheek.

Alex stuffed marshmallows in her mouth, the wheels turning. She was going crazy upstairs in her room. If only she could get out of the house! She bet Kevin's band was practicing in his garage right this minute.

Alex rinsed out her glass and set it in the sink. "I ache all over. Maybe if I sleep about ten hours, I can avoid getting the flu that's going around."

"An early night sounds good to me too." Grandma shrugged her shoulders and turned her neck from side to side. "After gardening today, I'm stiff as a board. While this soda bread bakes, I'm soaking my poor bones in the tub."

Excellent! Alex thought. "Good night, then." She kissed her grandmother's floury cheek.

Upstairs, Alex turned out the lights in her room and waited. Ten minutes later she heard Grandma come upstairs and run water in the tub, then close the bathroom door with a click.

The lighted dial on Alex's clock said 7:48. She had to get moving before Grandpa got home. Alex grabbed her denim jacket off the peg on the back of her door, sneaked out of her room, quietly closed her door behind her, then tiptoed down the hall. She paused outside the bathroom door. Grandma was singing "Amazing Grace" while splashing around in the water.

She glided downstairs, then out the front door. *Freedom!* The air was cool, making it an invigorating night to break out of jail. Alex reached for her bike, then changed her mind and leaned it back against the house. When Grandpa drove in, her bike couldn't be missing.

Half walking, half jogging, she headed in the direction of Kevin's house. The address he'd given her was only two blocks farther west than Morgan's house. The Gnosh was on the way, and Alex decided to stop for a soda. When she arrived at the restaurant at eight, Morgan was wiping off tables. Only three booths still held customers.

"Hey, what's up?" Morgan asked.

"Just out walking and wanted a Coke to go."

"Sure." While Morgan was getting the drink, Mrs. Cross emerged from the kitchen. "Looks pretty dead out here. Why don't you go on home, Morgan? We can close."

"Thanks, Mom. I'm pooped."

Alex sipped her Coke while Morgan got her jacket from the office, then they left. "Want to come home and watch a movie with me?" Morgan asked. "Maya's got a date, so we'd have the place to ourselves for a change."

"Maybe." Alex pretended to consider it as they crossed the street. Half a block later, Alex suddenly snapped her fingers. "I know what we can do!"

"What?"

"Kevin said his band practices at night in his garage. Want to go see? He kind of invited me."

"I don't know . . ." Morgan pulled her jacket collar up closer to her face. "I'm not supposed to just take off without asking."

Don't be a goody two shoes! Not now! Alex thought. "Let's just go for a short walk then."

"Like accidentally past Kevin's house?"

"I'm not even sure where he lives."

"Oh. Well, okay."

"Great." Alex turned at the next corner and gave Morgan a detailed account of Grandpa discovering Kevin's e-mails. "No wonder my mom ran away when she was only sixteen."

"It's hard to imagine," Morgan agreed. "That's barely more than a year older than we are now."

"Weird, huh?" Alex couldn't *imagine* dropping out of school and running off with a guy a year from now. Had her mom been terrified? She would be!

They shuffled along the sidewalk in silence. Suddenly Morgan stopped. "Listen."

A dog barked in the distance, a squirrel skittered up a nearby tree, and a car honked at the corner. But, Alex heard music. Band music.

"Gee, maybe Kevin's house *is* nearby," Alex said.

"You can drop the innocent act," Morgan said. "Where's he live?"

"Two-twenty-four Cedar," Alex said with a grin.

Morgan shook her head. "I'm surprised your grandpa lets you wander around town alone. He usually watches you like a hawk."

Alex shrugged, but said nothing. It was better that Morgan not know she'd sneaked out. Her best friend had developed such a tender conscience lately that she might feel compelled to bust Alex.

Three houses down was 224 Cedar, and sure enough, music echoed from inside the garage at the side of the two-story house. Alex's heart pounded painfully as they approached the garage. Would Kevin be glad to see her or had he only been polite by saying she could come? What if he'd invited *other* girls too?

Alex and Morgan peered through the glass in the side door. Alex spotted Kevin, whose back was turned, as he talked to the bass player. She didn't recognize the drummer, who wore a metallic-ball chain necklace with a big cross on it and a T-shirt advertising a band called Insyderz.

Alex's heart nearly burst when Kevin began to sing, his voice muted through the door. Alex could make out only a few words, something about "lonely hearts" and "after the pain comes joy." *Sad words,* Alex thought, yet she loved the music.

At the end of the song, Kevin turned to speak to the drummer and stared right into Alex's eyes. She jerked back, but it was too late. Smiling, he motioned for her to come in.

Alex pulled on Morgan's arm, but Morgan hung back. "You *have* to come in with me!" Alex said. "There are three guys, and I can't go in alone."

"The things I do for you," Morgan muttered. Head tucked down in the collar of her jacket, she followed her friend inside.

"Hi! Glad you could make it." Kevin's guitar hung from the strap around his neck.

"Uh, yeah, well." Alex was painfully aware of the other two boys' grins. She probably sounded like a stuttering, teenybopper groupie. She cleared her throat. "We were just walking by. I didn't realize you lived on *this* block."

Morgan's mouth fell open.

Kevin grinned. "Well, next time you can walk by on purpose then."

Alex grinned back. He'd said *next time* like it might become a regular thing!

"Here, meet the guys." Kevin pointed at the drummer. "That's Nick." Nick nodded and did a drum roll. "And that's Shonn." Peering closer, Alex recognized the bass player with the chops as one of their football jocks. Shonn winked and flashed his dimples. "Graham's usually on keyboard, but he had to work tonight."

"Hi." Alex was suddenly tongue-tied. "Please go ahead and practice. We'll stay out of the way."

"You guys mind having an audience?" Kevin asked.

"We'll take one when we can get one," Shonn called.

For the next twenty minutes, Morgan and Alex sat on a wooden crate and listened to them play and replay the opening to a new song Kevin had written. Alex's head pounded in rhythm with the drums, but it was worth it to hear Kevin sing.

More than once, he looked right at Alex, as if they were the only two people in the room.

Cardiac arrest, here I come, she thought.

Morgan elbowed her in the ribs. "I need to go. My folks will be home soon."

Alex nodded reluctantly. If she hurried, she could beat Grandpa home too. They stood and eased toward the door. When the song ended, Kevin hurried over. "Have to go already? I'm glad you could stop by. Come back again."

"We *will!*" Alex blushed at the eager tone in her voice. "You're really good," she rushed on. "You guys should cut a demo or go on tour."

"We're not *that* good yet but maybe someday. I have other plans before that."

"Really? Like what?"

"College for one thing. I want to get a foundation at a good music school, you know, so I can have teaching to fall back on before I try making it in a Christian band."

What a charming waste of talent and time, Alex thought. "We'd better go."

Kevin opened the door for them. "Bye. Oh, Morgan, I'm glad you could make it too."

"Thanks." Morgan ducked her head and hurried outside. They jogged the three blocks back to the Cross house, gasping by the time they arrived. The house was still dark. "I'm in luck," Morgan said, unlocking the kitchen door. "I beat them home."

"Thanks for going with me." With a wave, Alex set off down the street, afraid she'd been gone too long.

When she arrived home, it was just as she'd feared: Grandpa's car was parked in the driveway. She peeked in the living room window. He sat in his recliner, the daily newspaper gripped in his hands, but he peered over his reading glasses to watch the TV news. How was she going to get inside and up the stairs without him seeing her? She could wait till he went to bed, but then he'd lock the front and back doors and she'd have to break in.

Alex had to create a distraction. Sneaking around to the back of the house, she peered through the glass in the kitchen door. It was dark inside except for the blue light on the microwave. Alex raised her fist and pounded hard. Knees shaking, she waited, but nothing happened. She'd raised her fist to pound again when Grandpa suddenly appeared in the kitchen doorway and the light blazed on.

She jumped back off the steps and sprinted around to the front of the house. Alex opened the front door an inch. She could hear Grandpa in the kitchen calling, "Hey, who's out there?"

She slipped inside, closed the front door, and sped across the living room to the stairs. The kitchen door slammed just as Alex closed the stairs door. She waited, her knees weak and wobbling, but when nothing happened, she tiptoed upstairs, clutching the railing all the way.

Alex sneaked past her grandparents' bedroom door. It was closed, but light spilled from under the door. *Good.* Grandma was still awake. If Grandpa heard footsteps overhead he would just think it was Grandma.

Alex made it to her room and closed the door with a tiny click. She was safe! She crawled into bed still wearing her clothes and lay there thinking about Kevin and his singing and the cool band. It was too bad he didn't want to perform yet. They were really good!

Just then a brilliant idea flashed through her mind. Wow! Would it be possible? Why not? She tiptoed over to the computer and logged on in the dark, holding her breath during the squeaky beeps of connecting. A minute later she typed her message to Kevin.

Hey, thanks for playing for Morgan and me. I'm glad we stopped by. You were awesome. I just had a great idea. Remember I told you we're singing for the Mother's Day Banquet? What if your group played backup music for us? Wouldn't that blow everyone away?

Just then Maverick jumped in her lap and knocked her arm, causing her to type a bunch of gobbledegook.

"Maverick," Alex whined. "Look what you made me do." Maverick nudged her head under Alex's arm, purring loudly.

Alex began backspacing across the mistakes when her door

opened. Her grandfather's silhouette was outlined in the doorway. "I thought I heard voices," he said, coming into the room and reading over her shoulder.

Alex clicked the message box closed. "That's private!"

"Not while you live under my roof." Grandpa shook his head slowly. "I mean it, Alexandra. Stay away from that boy."

Alex clamped her jaws together and bit back angry words. She didn't dare open her mouth and infuriate Grandpa. It would be just like him to cut off her computer privileges then.

It was just a very good thing, Alex thought, that he couldn't read her mind.

chapter.7

The week dragged by for Alex. She sent Kevin three e-mails, but when he hadn't answered any of them by Wednesday, she stopped writing. Then a short e-mail on Thursday just said he'd been really busy, but he'd write more soon. She slumped back in disappointment. At least she could look forward to Karaoke Night, she thought. Maybe Kevin would come again.

But after school Friday, she discovered that Grandpa had volunteered her to baby-sit for a family at church with two little boys. They lived less than a block from Alex, and they needed her while they attended a wedding. They'd be late, after a reception and dance. Much too late for Alex to go to Karaoke Night.

"He didn't even ask me!" Alex complained to Grandma after school.

Grandma frowned. "He thought you'd be pleased to earn some extra money." Alex eyed Grandma skeptically. Was she really that naive? Grandpa wasn't doing her any *favors!* He was tying her down to make sure she didn't see Kevin at the Gnosh that night. Aggravated almost beyond endurance, Alex stomped off to read.

Half an hour later she heard Grandpa come in for supper. He'd been in the garage constructing wire cages for their tomato plants and brought one in to show Grandma how tall he was making them. Alex stood in the doorway and glared at his bent back while Grandma *oohed!* and *ahhed!* over his stupid tomato cages.

"Gee," Alex said, "can you make a bigger one?" Grandpa looked around, a puzzled expression on his face. "For *me*," she said sweetly. "You know. Tomatoes in cages. Granddaughters in cages. It's all the same!" She grabbed her book bag. "I'm going now, or I'll be late." Without another word, she trudged out the back door and headed down the street to baby-sit.

Alex hated baby-sitting. The tiny toddler and preschooler couldn't entertain themselves for five measly minutes. By the time they collapsed at ten in their bunk beds, she'd fed them hot dogs, cleaned up after them, bathed them, mopped the flooded bathroom, read a zillion bedtime stories, picked up their toys, fixed them a bedtime snack, then swept the kitchen floor. When the Teals finally arrived home, Alex took the money but declined a ride home. No way was she crawling into a car with Mr. Teal. His aftershave smelled like weed-killer.

At home, Alex quickly logged on. She had no e-mail, but when she clicked the TodaysGirls.com Web site, Bren, Maya, Amber, and Jamie were already chatting.

> **nycbutterfly:** hey there Alex. missed U @ the Gnosh 2nite
>
> **TX2step:** had to babysit. was it busy?
>
> **chicChick:** it was dead @ first. so we practiced a song 4 the mom's day banquet
>
> **TX2step:** what song?
>
> **faithful1:** it's called What If I Stumble? I had the sheet music. it's a cool song. u'll like it.
>
> **TX2step:** where's Morg?
>
> **nycbutterfly:** thought she was online in the kitchen.
>
> **rembrandt:** wish U could have practiced w/us. hey! Kevin showed up and asked about U, Alex

Alex's heart sped up. He had? Now she was doubly furious at her interfering grandfather. She could have seen Kevin tonight at the Gnosh! Alex bet Bren hadn't minded she wasn't there. Her flirting with Kevin still bugged Alex. Like did Bren have to act like every guy was in love with her?

> **nycbutterfly:** that reminds me. Alex, I found some good fashion sites 4 u. Try fashionforever.com and fashionsRU.com. they've got what's hot. they even

have an e-mail address where u can send fashion questions.

TX2step: why would I ask them ???????????

nycbutterfly: so u don't buy something that's out. U want to be in, don't u?

rembrandt: Gap and Old Navy web sites have got cute stuff! 2 much $ 4 me tho!

TX2step: u guys don't get it. I like how I look.

faithful1: u always look good, Alex. ignore them. just B yourself.

jellybean: Amber's right. leave Alex alone, u guys.

nycbutterfly: she's back! Is the fridge empty????

jellybean: haha. split a gut laughing.

nycbutterfly: shut up.

chicChick: but fine! we were only trying 2 help

In spite of her brave words, Alex felt depressed when she exited the chat room. Maya made her mad. Did she have to make Alex sound like a total loss? Like she needed their advice!

Still . . . it couldn't hurt to look. Despising herself for doing it, Alex checked out the fashion sites.

It didn't take her five minutes to see why they thought she needed radical help. Wearing baggy pants and tank tops was the only things she did right, according to the "fashion experts." She'd always prided herself on being her own person, and yet . . . now she'd met someone that she really wanted to impress. Would she have to look like the rest of the world to do it?

Even if she wanted to, Alex realized, she couldn't afford it. Her clothing "budget" was nonexistent. Where would the money come from for a floral poncho from the Gap ($48), a pleather jacket ($39), or snap-on faux fur jeans ($42)? Like she'd be caught dead in those! Even a T-shirt at the Gap cost $19.50!

Clicking over to a makeup and perfume site, Alex got side-tracked by a banner ad that ran across the top of her screen. The ad suggested sending your mother an electronic gift certificate for Mother's Day. Just being reminded of Mother's Day was an instant downer. Why didn't advertisers get a clue? Not everyone liked those ads! What about people who didn't have mothers anymore? Or people who didn't know their biological mothers? Alex bet that all that advertising just made a lot of people— including her—feel rotten.

Before giving up for the night, Alex clicked one last time on her e-mail icon and found a message from *kdean17.*

Hey, Tex! Sorry I missed you at the Gnosh tonight. I stopped to see you.

Alex grinned. He'd come specifically to see *her.*

The guys are glad to play backup music for the banquet. I told Amber tonight, and she said

you're singing **What If I Stumble?** Cool song.
Amber's loaning us her sheet music, so we can
make a practice tape if you want. I hope you had
a good night! See you later. Kevin.

That night Alex fell into bed exhausted by the Teal boys but
happier. At least she could sleep late the next day. She'd pulled
her shades all the way down. Hopefully the room would stay
pitch dark till noon.

It seemed her head had barely hit the pillow before her door flew
open with a bang. "Rise and shine!" Maya ordered, sailing into
Alex's bedroom. "We're here to rescue you." She whipped the
window shades up.

"Whuh—What?" Alex leaned up on one elbow. Morgan
hung back in the doorway, looking sheepish. "What're you
doing here?"

"I'm sorry," Morgan said quietly. "I tried to stop her."

Squinting at her bedside clock made Alex's head pound.
"Man! It's only 10:30."

"We've been up for hours." Maya dumped two bags on Alex's
bed, then turned in a slow circle. "So. This is your room."

"Yes," Alex snapped. "And what are you *doing* in it?"

"We will overlook your rude tone because we interrupted
your beauty sleep," Maya said, "but your grandmother told us to
come right up." She sat down on the bed, bouncing Alex's

throbbing head. She pulled clothing, still with tags on, out of colorful bags with handles. "Now feast your eyes! You know that new boutique down in Olde Edgewood?"

"No."

"Sure you do. It's by that coffeehouse and bookstore place."

"I don't shop there."

"Well, you will! Look at this stuff!" She pulled out shirts, a miniskirt, some short shorts, and jeans. "They let us take it on approval because our mom knows the manager. They're trying to compete with the businesses from the mall, I think, so we brought the fashion show to you!"

"You're doing a fashion show for me?"

"No! *You're* going to model everything, then keep what you like. The next time Kevin sees you, he won't even recognize you."

Maya cleared a place on her desk. "We brought makeup samples and stuff to fix your hair." Maya piled lipstick, blush, eyeliners, eye shadow, and spot concealer on the desk. From another larger bag came mousse, gel, and hairspray.

"But—but—" Alex looked from Maya to Morgan and back again. Maya wore her "steamroller" look, and Morgan mouthed the words, "I'm really sorry!" Alex collapsed on her pillows. Why fight it? She'd get rid of Maya faster if she let her do her thing.

An hour later, Alex had tried on every piece of overpriced clothing. Maya loved the short shorts, but Alex knew Grandpa would hit the roof if she appeared in those. Anyway, they made her feel way too exposed. Same thing for the miniskirt.

"You don't want to look geekish," Maya said. "But you don't want to look like you're trying to be 'all that' either."

"Whatever." Alex scowled at Morgan, but Morgan refused to meet her eyes. Just wait! Morgan was going to get an earful later for not stopping her sister! Would she ever get done? One of Alex's glittery fake nails had dried on crooked, and Maya wasn't finished with her makeup. She'd applied licorice-lids eyeliner and strawberry-squeal lip liner, but the lashrageous mascara and pinktastic blush were still left.

When she finally finished at 12:30, Maya stood back, hands on hips, and whistled. "You're hot!" she said like she'd worked some miracle. "Go check yourself out."

Alex dragged herself down the hall to the full-length mirror on the back of the bathroom door. She stared at her reflection, blinked, and stared some more. *A miracle?* she thought. *More like a nightmare!*

Admittedly Maya had tried to find things she thought Texans would love. With her trimmed bell-bottom jeans, Alex wore a fur-trimmed poncho. On top of her moussed, gelled, stiff hair sat a purple vinyl cowboy hat. Alex had drawn the line at a rose from the body art tattoo kit. With the makeup she looked about eighteen, which she didn't mind, and she was quite sure they were right about one thing: Kevin would never recognize her. She didn't recognize herself.

Alex forced herself to smile when she walked back to her bedroom. "It's a real transformation all right." She removed the cowboy hat, then the poncho, and put them back in the sacks.

"Don't you want to keep them?" Maya asked in astonishment. "You look so cool."

"I'll think about it," Alex said, knowing full well that even if she liked the clothes she could never afford them. "If I decide to buy them, I know where the boutique is now."

"Well, if you're sure . . ."

"I'm sure." Alex changed clothes, grateful to get into her oversize shirt and pants. She handed them the bags of makeup and clothes, then walked them downstairs. "I'm really sorry," Morgan whispered again before they left.

Alex headed straight back upstairs to the bathroom. She scrubbed her face raw. Her eyes stung from the soap after scrubbing off the lavender-glamender eye shadow. She grabbed her brush, but she couldn't yank it through her stiff tangled hair. Finally she bent over the tub to shampoo out the gel and mousse so her hair could return to its natural state.

Finally, standing in front of the mirror, she examined her oversize clothes, flaming red face, and wet frizzy hair. Alex shook her head dismally. Why even try?

chapter.8

That night Alex watched TV till nine with her grandparents, bored stiff by the black-and-white rerun on public television. If only they'd turn in early and she could sneak out again to listen to Kevin's band. Lying on the floor, Alex dozed off but was jolted awake by the phone. She grabbed it. It was Harry Short.

"Coach, what's up?"

"Give me your grandfather fast."

"Just a sec." Alex stretched the long cord over to Grandpa's recliner. "It's for you."

Her grandfather listened a moment, frowning. "When did it happen?" He nodded. "I'll be right there."

"What is it?" Grandma asked when he hung up.

"Broken water pipe in the church basement. Pastor just found it and Harry's there."

Grandma pulled on her sweater. "I'll come too. I imagine there's a soggy mess to clean up."

They both looked at Alex. "I'm going to bed early," she said, squashing a tinge of guilt. No way would she miss this golden opportunity to see Kevin.

The minute their car was out of sight, she grabbed her jacket and hopped on her bike. She wouldn't stay long, but Kevin *had* said he'd make a backup music tape so they could practice. If worse came to worst and she got caught, she could produce the tape and say Kevin had called after they left.

It was too bad Grandpa's narrow-minded attitude made all this sneaking around necessary, but a girl had to do what a girl had to do. Smiling, Alex pedaled down the street. It was high time things went her way.

When she parked her bike outside Kevin's garage, she could hear the band playing. She closed her eyes to listen more closely. Was that the music for their banquet song? It sounded like the one Amber had been singing the other day. Alex slipped inside, and the words were suddenly clear.

What if I stumble, what if I fall?
What if I lose my step and I make fools of us all?
Will the love continue
When my walk becomes a crawl?
What if I stumble, and what if I fall?

What if I stumble, what if I fall?
You never turn in the heat of it all.
What if I stumble, what if I fall?

At the end of the song Nick stood and stretched his lanky frame to its full six feet. "Sorry. Gotta run. I'll see you guys." He left his sticks on his drum, turned, and spotted Alex. "Hey, Kevin, you've got company." He ran a hand over his spiky bleached hair, but it didn't move.

Kevin turned and grinned. "Hi! I'm sorry, but we're done for the night."

"That's okay. I heard the last song." Suddenly embarrassed, she stammered out, "Um, you said, that is, you were making a tape? I mean, for the banquet song?" Alex felt her face flush. "I was wondering if it was done so I could start practicing."

"Right. We finished it an hour ago." He got the cassette from a tape player sitting on top of a wooden stool. "Here it is. The quality's not the best, but it'll work for practicing."

"Thanks. This'll really help."

Shonn put up his bass guitar and Nick covered his drums. Shonn scratched his goatee and winked again at Alex as he and Nick left. Graham—who looked like a model with his perfect dark skin and eyes—was right behind them.

Kevin handed her Amber's sheet music. "This might be an unusual choice for Mother's Day, but I think it's a cool song."

"Amber picked it actually, but I do like the music." Alex sang a line, hoping Kevin would be impressed. "I've never played in a band though. I wouldn't have the rhythm."

Kevin cocked his head to one side and studied her. "I don't believe that. It's a lot easier than it looks. I bet you'd do fine on a guitar." He went over and picked up Shonn's bass guitar. "The bass chords are pretty simple." He slipped the strap around her neck. "Shonn won't mind. Hold it here," he said, positioning her fingers.

With Kevin standing so close, Alex barely breathed. His face was only inches from hers as he showed her how to strum and change chords. Actually, she remembered quite a bit from playing with her dad's old guitar, but no way would she admit that and end her private music lesson! Let him be impressed with how fast she caught on.

"Let's put the two sounds together," Kevin said ten minutes later. "I'll sing and play the lead, and you do those simple bass chords."

Alex smiled nervously. "I'll try."

They faced each other, and Alex watched Kevin's hands in order to match his rhythm. She hit a couple of sour chords, but then found the right ones. At the sound of Kevin's mellow voice, Alex feared her legs would melt and leave her in a puddle on the cement floor.

Do they see the fear in my eyes?
Are they so revealing?

This time I cannot disguise
All the doubt I'm feeling
What if I stumble, what if I fall?
What if I lose my step and I make fools of us all?
Will the love continue
When my walk becomes a crawl?
What if I stumble, and what if I fall?

While Alex didn't really understand the message, she could have listened to Kevin sing for hours. Sometimes he closed his eyes, like he was praying. Other times he gazed into her eyes. Alex couldn't believe she was standing in this incredible guy's garage, playing guitars while he sang to her. If it was a dream, she didn't want to wake up. He was the kindest guy she'd ever known. His being a Christian was something she could learn to live with.

At the end of the song, Alex reluctantly set down the bass guitar.

"Do you have to go?" Kevin asked.

"I don't want to be in your way."

"You're not. You can stay longer." Kevin pretended to block her escape. "I love a captive audience."

"Well, okay." Alex figured her grandparents would be busy with the church's plumbing mess for at least a couple of hours.

So for another hour and a half she practiced on the bass, following Kevin's lead on several different songs, then the banquet song again. Alex sighed, wishing she could stay forever. But unless she left now, her grandparents might beat her home. She picked up the tape and sheet music. "I'd better get going."

"Okay. Well, I'm glad you could come over." Kevin walked outside with her and waved as she coasted down his driveway and headed home.

Alex was already in bed when she heard her grandparents drive in. She'd been listening to the practice tape, following the lyrics on Amber's sheet music while strumming chords on an imaginary bass guitar. She pressed STOP on her tape player and snapped off her light. Let Grandpa assume she'd gone to bed early. What he didn't know couldn't hurt him—*or her*.

Sunday afternoon, Alex stopped at the Cross house. "Where's Morgan?" Alex asked when Maya answered the door.

"Reading out back." Maya studied Alex from head to toe. "Our makeover didn't last long." She grinned. "Did you turn into a pumpkin at midnight?"

Alex gritted her teeth. With one little comment, Maya could make her feel like a bag lady. Ignoring her, Alex walked around back and found Morgan reclining in a lounge chair, an open book across her stomach. "Hey, lazy girl," Alex called, pulling another chair close to her friend's.

"Hi!" Morgan shaded her eyes as she looked up. "Doesn't the sun feel great? Can you believe school will be over in a month? I'm not going to do anything in June but read in the sun."

Alex sighed deeply.

Morgan turned toward her friend. "That was a huge sigh. What's up?"

Alex stared around the Crosses' backyard, from the apple trees filled with pink and white blossoms to the border of red and gold tulips. "Mom's not coming up for Mother's Day after all. She won't even ask for the time off."

"But I thought—Never mind."

Alex picked at a hangnail. "I'm *sick* of being understanding all the time. She hasn't even said when I get to go back home."

"I'm sorry, Alex. I bet you miss your family. I know I would." Morgan shifted to face her. "Any way I can help?"

"Nobody can help."

They lapsed into silence, and Alex lay back in her chair. A gentle breeze ruffled the pink apple blossoms overhead, and petals floated down on her like fragrant snow. It was a peaceful setting, but her heart was full of turmoil. Just then Alex spotted something hanging from a twig above her head. She stood up on her tiptoes and gently pulled the end of the branch down. "Look. A cocoon."

Morgan peered close. "Actually it's a chrysalis."

"Whatever. See that crack in it? A butterfly's trying to get out! I think it's stuck." Alex slid her thumbnail into the crack.

"Don't!"

Alex paused. "Why not?"

"When I was ten I found a chrysalis like this one where the butterfly looked stuck. I cut the chrysalis open with some scissors.

The butterfly came out easy, but its shriveled wings never unfolded. The butterfly crawled around with a swollen body and shriveled wings till it died."

"A butter*flop* then, not a butter*fly*."

"Not funny." Morgan shook her head. "I asked my science teacher about it. He said after the caterpillar turns into a butterfly in the chrysalis, its body swells to crack the shell." She pointed. "Having to squash through that tiny slit is part of the process. It squeezes fluid out of the butterfly's fat body into its wrinkled-up wings so it can fly."

"My, my," Alex said, "aren't you the little science wizard?"

Morgan shrugged. "The struggle's part of its life cycle." Morgan hesitated. "Don't take this wrong, but Coach said that struggles are sometimes what we need in our own life cycles too."

"I don't think so! We're hardly butterflies."

"No, but if we went through life with no problems, we'd never be as strong as we are after dealing with them."

"Easy for you to say," Alex snapped, glancing at Morgan's fancy house where she lived with both her parents.

"Sorry. I just meant that working through the thing with your mom could make you stronger. You know, like when a butterfly is forced to break out by itself."

"I'd rather skip the hassles, thank you very much."

"Okay, but keeping all that anger inside will hurt you. Forgiving could set you free to fly."

"Oh please!" Alex stood abruptly. "I've got to go. I didn't come for a sermon." She left without another word.

The week dragged on forever. It was only nine days till Mother's Day, but since her mom wasn't coming, it hardly mattered anymore. Alex counted the days till Friday instead. If Grandpa arranged another baby-sitting job this week, he could take it himself. Alex was going to the Gnosh!

Thursday afternoon was unusually warm, and Alex nearly dozed off in her biology and math classes. If she hoped to write her literature paper that night, she'd better catch some zzz's after school.

At home Grandma and Grandpa were hunched over a huge crossword puzzle at the kitchen table. Grandpa filled in the blanks while Grandma looked up clues in her special crossword dictionary. They barely spoke to Alex as she grabbed a raisin cookie and headed up to her bedroom. Alex hoped she was never so old that her biggest excitement for the week was a crossword puzzle.

Upstairs in her stuffy bedroom she opened the window. She tossed her backpack on the bed, then did a double take. She reached for a shopping bag on her bed with the words CELE-BRATE SAN ANTONIO! on it. Had it come from her mom in the mail? She opened the bag, then whipped around when a movement behind her bedroom door startled her.

"Surprise!"

"Mom!" Alex shrieked. She rushed at her mother, knocking her off balance by throwing her arms around her. "I can't believe it!"

Her mom laughed and hugged her back, tight. "Believe it, honey! I flew in this morning."

"Talk about a shock!" She stepped back but hung on to her mom's hand. "Grandma and Grandpa acted so innocent downstairs!"

"I asked them to let me surprise you."

Alex studied her mom, dressed in neatly pressed khakis and a white v-neck sweater. She wore her favorite pair of earrings—tiny round pearls—and her long hair was pulled back by a large barrette. Except that they were both petite, no one would guess they were related. "How'd you get time off? And the money for a plane ticket?"

They sat on the bed, arms around each other's waists. "My new boss announced that the office would be closed this week for inventory. I could have helped with inventory, but I asked to come see you instead, and he said sure!"

"But the money?"

"You can thank Grandma for that. Mom was so psyched up about you girls singing for the Mother's Day Banquet that she sent me money to come home."

"How long can you stay?"

"Nine days. Through Mother's Day, then I fly back on Monday."

"I still can't believe it."

"Won't it be fun sharing my old room?" she asked, singing a light tune as she moved to unpack. Alex nodded, soaking up the sound of her mother's musical voice. Oh, how she'd missed that.

That night they talked nonstop through supper. Alex barely tasted her food, even though Grandma had fixed her daughter's favorite meal: Dublin coddle made of spicy sausages and potatoes, plus apple fritters for dessert. Alex would have been content to just sit and stare at her mom all evening. It all seemed so unreal.

"So tell me, honey, how long have you and your friends had a singing group?"

"We don't, not really," Alex explained. "We just sang together on Karaoke Night once at the Gnosh."

"The Gnosh? Now that's Morgan's family's restaurant?"

"Actually, it's called the Gnosh Pit. I can't wait for you to meet my friends." *Including Kevin,* Alex thought. "You could stop by for a minute tomorrow for Karaoke Night."

"I *would* like to meet Morgan and her parents since you've talked about them so much. But even if I don't make it, you feel free to join your friends anyway."

Grandpa cleared his throat noisily. "Alex doesn't need to go to the Gnosh again with all those wild teenagers."

"You're not my parent, and it's hardly wild." Alex arched one eyebrow. "Besides, Mom said I could go, didn't you?"

Suddenly they resembled a game of freeze tag. No one at the table moved. Alex waited for her mom to stick up for her.

"Karaoke at a family restaurant sounds like fun," her mom said softly. "I don't see any harm in Alex going."

Grandpa dropped his fork. It bounced against his plate, then flipped on the floor. "You didn't see any harm in your *own* activities when you were Alexandra's age either. Do you want history repeating itself?"

Alex gasped. Two bright spots of red appeared on her mom's cheeks, but the rest of her face turned a sickly white.

chapter.9

Do you want history repeating itself? Grandpa's harsh words to Alex's mom hung in the air. "You might not think it's so harmless if you saw the mail Alex receives from an older boy she met there." He pushed back his chair and stomped outside.

Grandma reached across the table and patted her daughter's arm. "Don't be upset, Gail. He didn't mean anything by it."

Ha! Alex thought. *He meant exactly what he said.*

Alex's mom rubbed her arms as if she were cold. "I guess that tension between us is still there."

"Don't let it spoil your visit," Grandma begged.

Alex nodded. "That's right, Mom. He treats me like that all the time." Noticing her grandmother's stricken face, she added, "I'm sorry, Grandma, but you know it's true."

"What's all this about mail from a boy?"

"Just e-mail. Grandpa saw a stupid Love Quiz I took on the Internet. He thought it was from Kevin, but it wasn't."

"He can jump to a lot of conclusions," her mom agreed. She tapped Alex on the arm. "So. When do I get to meet this Kevin?"

"You might if you come to Karaoke Night tomorrow."

They carried the leftovers to the kitchen, then scraped, washed, and dried the dishes. Through the kitchen window, Alex saw Grandpa hoeing furiously in the vegetable garden. What a crab.

That night Alex and her mom talked till nearly midnight, whispering in bed long after they turned out the lights. Alex hadn't felt that close to her mom in over a year. Alex was relieved that things sounded better at home. Since there were only five weeks of school left, they'd need to talk about how she'd get home in June. She couldn't wait.

Except for one thing. She'd just met Kevin, and he was so . . . crush-worthy.

The next night was warm, and Alex and her mom walked to the Gnosh Pit. "I'm not going to stay long, but I do want to meet your friends," her mom said.

"I want them to meet you too." Glancing sideways, Alex realized that her trim mother, dressed in jeans and a sweater set with her long hair in a ponytail, could pass for a college coed.

The restaurant was only half full when they arrived. Alex introduced her mom to Morgan's parents; then Amber, Bren, Maya; and Morgan motioned for Alex and her mom to join them. Her mom was a beauty, if Alex said so herself, and she proudly introduced her.

"This is your *mom?*" Maya asked. "Well, now!"

Alex squeezed into the booth beside her mom and smiled smugly. Now Maya could stop looking at her with such pity.

Since this was the fourth Karaoke Night, the Gnosh soon filled to capacity. Jared started the night's singing. Alex grinned at his "Flying Purple People Eater" song as he gyrated up front.

When the song ended, Alex's mom said, "I think I'm going to head home and leave you here with your friends."

Suddenly Morgan elbowed Alex in the ribs. "He's here!" she hissed.

Alex leaned around her mom to see. Kevin stood just inside the front door, looking over the crowd. When he spotted Alex, he headed to their booth while three guys sang some football song interspersed with dumb cheers.

"Hi, Kevin." Alex felt herself blush. "I'd like you to meet my mom, Gail Diaz. She flew up from Texas yesterday. Mom, this is Kevin."

"Hello, Kevin." Her mom held out a tanned hand. "I hear your group is playing backup for the girls at the banquet."

He shook her hand. "Looking forward to it. Amber chose a song we really like—"

He was drowned out by Beach Boys music blaring over the sound system. He waited while four high school boys belted out, "'Wish they all could be California girls!'"

When the song was over, Kevin said, "Guess I'd better go park it. Nice meeting you, Mrs. Diaz. I hope you enjoy your visit."

"Here, take my seat. I'm heading home early." She stood up and smiled at each girl in turn. "Nice to meet you girls. Can't wait to hear you sing!" Then she winked knowingly at Alex and left.

"Your mom's cool," Bren said. "I would never have guessed you were related!"

Alex fumed, but said nothing.

Bren reached over and touched Kevin's arm. "Do you think they look alike?"

"What difference does it make?" Alex snapped.

Kevin slid in beside Alex. "Is she here just to visit?" His voice dropped so that only Alex could hear him. "Or are you going home with her to Texas?"

Alex glanced sideways. He sounded like he cared! "I'll finish the school year here, but yeah, when school's out, I'll move home."

There was a long silence. "I'm glad for you, honest." Kevin bumped her shoulder with his. "But I'm selfish too. I was hoping you'd be around this summer."

Alex hoped he couldn't hear the pounding of her heart. She wished she could agree with him, but she couldn't. No matter how much she liked him, her heart's desire was to go home. If only she could be in two places at once! "There's always e-mail, and I bet someday your band will play the Texas circuit."

"Hey, you two, no fair whispering!" Bren said when the next song ended.

Alex ignored her, but it grew harder with each song to hear Kevin talking, even though he sat right beside her. Alex regretted that, but on the other hand, the noise made it impossible for Bren to flirt with him.

Fifteen minutes later, Jamie rushed over to their table. "It's about time," Bren snapped. "I want some onion rings and a diet cola, and—"

"Sorry, I didn't come to take your order. I'm swamped!" Jamie's hair stood up as if she'd raked her fingers through it. "Morgan, your dad wants you and Alex to help bus tables for an hour or so. We don't have enough people working for this crowd."

Alex gave Jamie a pleading look. Here she was, sitting next to Kevin, and they wanted her to pick up dirty dishes! *I don't think so!* Besides, no way was she leaving Kevin alone with Bren.

"Come on, you guys," Jamie said. "We need you now."

This is so unfair! Alex screamed inwardly.

Kevin stood to let Alex out. "Come on. I'll help too. It'll go faster. Besides, I'd rather bus tables than sit here without you."

Alex's mouth fell open. "Uh, I know the Crosses would appreciate it," she finally said, grinning at the shocked look on Bren's face.

For the next hour, Alex worked side by side with Kevin to clear away dirty dishes. Alex couldn't remember the last time she'd had that much fun! She loved the curious stares they got as they moved from table to table. What a guy! It really *was* too bad she'd be moving back to Texas so soon.

Alex slept better that night than she had in six months, in spite of having to share the double bed with her mom. Her dreams were an odd combination of singing cats playing guitars, purple cowboy hats, and fried chicken. When she woke up late Saturday morning, her mom's side of the bed was empty and her stomach was growling.

Alex padded barefoot downstairs and heard voices coming from the kitchen. "So you're really all right?" Grandma asked.

"Yes, Mom. Really." Alex's mom sounded firm. "He's hardly drinking at all anymore. It'll be fine."

"But will *you* be fine?"

"You worry too much. Carlos is a good man. He just has some problems that we need to work through. But it is truly getting better."

"Oh, Gail, I hope so."

Alex hugged herself and felt like shouting. Her parents were working things out! She'd get to go home the minute school was out for sure. Even with Kevin in Edgewood, she couldn't wait.

"Morning, everyone." Alex entered the kitchen, kissed her mom and grandma, then pushed an English muffin down in the toaster.

Grandma poured more coffee for her daughter and herself. "I understand your young man's group is playing for the banquet."

"Yes, well, Kevin's hardly mine." Alex leaned against the counter. "How'd you like him, Mom?"

"I thought he was very nice. Very respectful. And *very* cute."

"Mom!"

"Sweetie, I'm old, not blind."

Alex giggled. "Yeah, he is pretty awesome."

Alex, her mom, and her grandma spent the day looking at old photo albums, spreading them across the living room floor. After hours of poring over the pictures, they all complained of aching backs, but no one really minded. They laughed and shared memories all day.

By ten that night, the house was still. Even Alex's mom was sound asleep, curled up with her face toward the wall. A gentle breeze stirred the yellow gingham curtains at the window. *Perfect,* Alex thought. She could leave the back door unlocked, sneak over to Kevin's band practice, then come home and crawl back in bed with no one the wiser.

She slipped out of bed, grabbed her jacket off its hook, then opened the bedroom door and pulled it shut behind her.

Meeoww!

Maverick's tail got caught in the door when she tried to follow Alex. "Oh, Maverick. I'm so sorry," she whispered. Alex scratched Maverick's chin and ears to calm her down, watching to make sure her mom didn't stir. Alex pushed Maverick back into the bedroom and quickly closed the door. Tiptoeing, she groped her way down the stairs in the dark.

In the kitchen, she turned on the tiny stove light and pulled on her running shoes. Her perfect day was about to get even better! She snapped off the stove light, let herself out the back door, then wheeled her bike away from the house. She nudged the kickstand up, swung one leg over, and hopped on.

At that moment, her mom's voice pierced the still night air.

"Alex!" she called from the upstairs window. "Where are you going?"

Alex froze.

"Come back inside right now."

Alex looked up at the dark window. "I will. Stop hollering." The last thing she needed was Grandpa waking up. She could handle her mom. After all, her mom had run away to have a life when she was Alex's age. But Grandpa? He'd nail her for sure.

Sighing, Alex trudged back inside the dark kitchen, closing the door behind her. Without warning, the ceiling light flashed on. Across the room stood her mom in her bathrobe—right next to Grandpa McGee.

"Well, young lady?" Grandpa asked.

Alex gulped. "Well what? I went outside for some fresh air." She kicked off her shoes and waited for her mother to jump in and help her.

"Where were you going, honey?" her mom asked quietly.

"I told you. I—"

"Were you meeting Kevin?" she asked even more quietly.

Alex frowned. "Well, yes, I was going to his house." Arms crossed in defiance, she glared at her grandfather. "It's his fault, Mom. If Grandpa had let Kevin come over like he wanted to, I wouldn't have to do this."

Grandpa shook his head slowly. "I didn't make you sneak out. Alexandra, you're grounded. Except for school and church, you're not to leave this house."

"You can't tell me that!" Alex sputtered. "You don't understand anything! You never understood Mom either! Right, Mom?"

Her mom collapsed at the kitchen table. "That may be true, but we're talking about *your* behavior, Alex. I have to agree with your grandpa. For sneaking out, you should be grounded."

Alex gasped. "Mom! I bet you used to do this!"

"Yes, I did, and I wish I hadn't." She glanced briefly at Grandpa. "I really wish I hadn't."

Alex burst into angry tears that embarrassed her, and she pushed between them to take the stairs two at a time. In her room, she ripped off her jacket, then grabbed the comforter and her pillow for a makeshift bed on the floor. No way would she share a bed with that traitor downstairs!

Her mom spoke to her when she finally came upstairs, but Alex refused to answer or get off the floor. Finally her mom gave up, closed the window, and crawled into bed.

The next morning Alex was stiff and sore from sleeping on the floor, but she pretended she'd slept wonderfully. At church she walked way ahead of her family to the pew near the front where Grandpa insisted they sit. Dropping into the pew, she slid down low in the seat, her knees resting against the pew just ahead. Grandpa hated when she slouched like that. She'd worn her baggiest, grungiest clothes, too, just to aggravate him.

She sat alone, waiting for the service to start, while the organist played two hymns. Once Alex glanced over her shoulder and was surprised to see her mom talking with Kevin at the back of the church. *Surely* her mom wouldn't tell him she'd been caught sneaking out! Alex let her hair fall forward to hide her face, but she peered out through the strands to watch them. Kevin was nodding while her mom talked. Alex frowned as her mom reached into her purse and handed Kevin a long envelope. What in the world?

A few minutes later her mom slipped in at the end of the pew, leaving Grandpa sitting between them. Alex slouched farther and pretended to sleep during the service. That always burned Grandpa. After the sermon and final hymn, Alex yawned and stood, casually scanning the church, but she couldn't find Kevin. She shuffled down the center aisle behind her mom, who was stopped every three feet by old ladies Grandma's age who had to welcome her back and get her whole life story. "Let me *out* of here," Alex muttered.

But when she and her mom reached the parking lot, Alex wanted to disappear back inside. Kevin was talking with Amber, but when he noticed Alex, he broke away and headed toward her, grinning. Alex was helpless to warn him.

Grandpa stepped between them. "Excuse me, young man. I want a word with you."

Kevin halted, glancing uncertainly from Alex to Grandpa and back. Alex stepped forward, but Grandpa put out his arm to stop her.

"What is it, sir?" Kevin asked.

"I'd like to know how many times Alex has been to your house."

Kevin blinked. "Sure. Twice."

"Twice."

"Yes, sir."

"So last night would have been three times?"

"Last night?" Kevin brushed a hand over his hair. "I don't know what you're talking about. I didn't even talk to Alex last night."

Grandpa moved within two feet of Kevin. "When you came calling, I said you were too old for my granddaughter. Having her sneak out to meet you late at night is too serious to ignore."

Kevin stepped around Grandpa to face Alex. "You sneaked out when you came to hear us practice before?"

Alex stared at the white gravel but finally nodded.

"And you lied about it?"

His words stung. "It's not a big deal," she whispered.

"Yes, it is. You knew it was wrong."

Alex gasped, and her heart skipped a beat. Was Kevin on *their* side? For a minute there, Alex had almost been sorry she'd sneaked out, but not anymore. She gritted her teeth, then pivoted on her heel and stalked across the gravel parking lot. She'd *walk* home.

chapter.10

Alex stalked away from the church parking lot. She'd never been so hurt or humiliated in her whole life. Having Grandpa question Kevin was bad enough. But Kevin had turned and blamed her! He hadn't even asked for her side of the story. An unexpected sob caught in her throat.

Alex took a very long way home, hoping they'd eat dinner without her if she was late enough. By the time she'd walked half an hour, she was sorry she'd given Kevin the silent treatment at church and stomped off. It wasn't his fault she'd tried to sneak out and got caught. He'd never do something like that, Alex was sure. After calming down, she had a sinking feeling in the pit of her stomach that she'd blown it permanently. All she'd ever wanted was for Kevin to like her.

She warred with her feelings the whole way home. Yes, she

knew deep down that Grandpa cared about her and didn't want her to go wild and ruin her life. Still, did he have to butt in all the time? He had no right to tell Kevin about last night or even to ground her.

And did Kevin have to take sides with Grandpa, of all people? How could he? Sure, it was probably wrong to lie about where she was going, but Kevin had no idea how it felt to live with Grandpa. It was a maximum-security prison.

Even so, what Kevin thought of her mattered. A *lot*.

When she finally walked into the house, no one asked where she'd been. Mom and Grandma hurried to get the roast, potatoes, and carrots out of the oven where they were staying warm. Grandpa kept them waiting while he folded the Sunday paper and put his reading glasses in their case before joining them at the head of the table.

Alex stared at her plate while Grandpa said grace. Throughout dinner, she listened to her mom and grandma make limp conversation. She thought about what Kevin had told her about not staying mad, but it was so hard! Still . . . she truly wanted to be the kind of girl he would admire. On her walk home, she'd decided to be calm and nice no matter *what*. To help her get through dinner, Alex pretended Kevin was sitting right beside her at the table, watching and listening to every word she said.

"Wasn't it nice seeing your friend Linda after all these years?" Grandma asked brightly.

Alex's mom reached for the salt and pepper. "Linda's barely

changed at all. I can't believe she has four kids! She said one's in your grade, Alex."

Alex forced herself to look interested. "His name's Chad." *And he's a real jerk,* she thought. *Don't be fooled because he goes to church.*

Grandma smiled, obviously relieved that Alex was making an effort. "Is he a friend of yours?"

"Not really." That Chad was such a creep. "He's in my lit class, but he doesn't say much." *Except mean, rotten things about other people,* she thought. "I'm sure he's very nice though." Alex stuffed her mouth with roast beef to keep from saying what she really thought. This "no hard feelings" stuff was hard work.

Grandma tapped Grandpa's arm. "You could ask Chad and his father to help with the cleanup in the church basement."

Alex choked at that suggestion and grabbed her glass of milk to wash down the meat. She ate the rest of her dinner in silence, anxious to escape.

After helping with dishes, Alex headed upstairs to the computer. She'd e-mail Kevin and apologize for stomping off in a huff. But when she clicked her e-mail icon, she already had mail from him.

Alex: I'm sorry for lecturing you at church instead of listening to you. Please forgive me. Ephesians 4:32 says to be kind and loving to each other; to forgive each other just as God

forgave you in Christ. I'll try to do better, but you can NOT sneak out and lie to your family anymore. That was wrong. I hope we're still friends. Kevin.

Alex sat back, flooded with mixed emotions. Kevin had apologized, but he still thought she was wrong. Did he have to include a Bible verse for everything? Didn't he have a mind of his own? Anyone with a strong enough will could forgive on his own. Hadn't she just proved that at dinner? "Fake it till you make it" was her motto. She didn't need God's help to do that.

She didn't print out his e-mail or answer it. She didn't know what to say.

At school on Monday, she hadn't been at the lunch table for two minutes before Maya started. "Couldn't you make the gel work?" she asked. "I showed you how to use it."

Alex seethed at the implication that her own natural hair looked bad. She swallowed her bite of mystery meat, then forced herself to smile sweetly. "My mom's still here. We were talking this morning, and I lost track of time. I'll try the gel tomorrow." *Like over my dead body.*

"Use the hairspray too. It'll help."

Alex felt her jaw go rigid. "What would I ever do without your expert advice?" she asked, her voice dripping sugar.

Morgan glanced sharply at her but said nothing. Maya, however, jumped right in. "Did you decide which clothes to buy? Get your mom to pay for them while she's here. I told that boutique owner you'd be in this week."

"Thank you for doing that, Maya." Alex concentrated on breathing in through her nose and out through her mouth. She'd heard it was supposed to help you calm yourself. This forgiveness junk took so much energy! She might be smiling on the outside, but her stomach was coated with acid. "Maybe I could get an outfit like yours." Alex studied Maya's lavender miniskirt and tiny T-shirt with purple flowers. *I wouldn't wear that to a dogfight.*

When the lunch bell finally rang, Alex jumped up, relieved to escape her friends. While she wanted to hang with them, she resented all this "help" in "fixing" her.

Morgan caught up with her at the cafeteria door. "What was all that about?"

"What?"

"Being all nicey-nice to Maya about your clothes and hair."

"You ought to understand that. You're big on forgiveness."

"Is *that* what that was? Sounded more like sarcasm to me."

"Okay," Alex said, forestalling another lecture, "so I don't have it down perfectly." Alex shifted her bag to her back. "See ya later."

After school that day Alex found her mom upstairs folding laundry. Socks and underwear and pajamas were piled high on the bed. Alex avoided her mom's hug but moved to help fold clothes. She could be polite, but having her mom take Grandpa's side Saturday night was still hard to swallow.

"Where's Grandma and Grandpa?"

"Church. Mom's working with her banquet committee on table decorations, and Dad's doing some plumbing. If you finish the socks, I'll see if the last load is dry."

"Okay." Alex gathered a pile of socks to match. As her mom went downstairs, Alex heard her grandparents' car pull into the driveway. She watched from her upstairs window as her grandfather emerged first, then hurried to open Grandma's door and help her out. Alex shook her head. How could Grandpa be so gentle with Grandma, yet so tough on her?

After finishing the socks, Alex decided to grab a Coke. Downstairs, the living room was deserted, but she could hear voices coming from the porch through the open window. Alex paused when she heard her name.

"I'm glad Alex is better today," Grandma said.

"Me too. That encounter in the parking lot had to be embarrassing."

"You've had your share of embarrassing moments, too, haven't you?" Grandma said softly.

Alex's mom was quiet for a moment. "Yes, with Dad and Carlos both. Don't get me wrong. Things are going better, but some days are still hard."

"Will it be easier when Alex comes home?"

"Eventually, yes." A wicker chair scraped the wooden porch.

"Mom, I need to ask you a big favor." She paused. The silence dragged on, and Alex moved closer to the open window. When she finally spoke, her mom's voice was low. "I need you to understand something. I can't have Alex come home for a while yet. I need more time to be sure that things are stable enough for her to come back. If it didn't work out, I couldn't put her through another terrible time." Alex heard footsteps then, pacing back and forth across the porch. "Can you keep Alex for the coming summer, maybe even next fall? I'm just not ready to add her back into the mix yet."

Alex gasped, then clenched her fists. It couldn't be true! With a trembling hand, she jerked open the living room door and stepped out on the porch. "I heard that!" she cried. "What kind of mother are you? You don't care about me at all!"

"Alex, honey!"

"Don't *Alex, honey* me! I'll never forgive you for this, not as long as I live!"

"Let me explain. You don't understand."

"I understand plenty! You don't want me back! I'd be in the way. You don't want me to come home!" Alex stormed back inside, slammed the door, and stumbled, sobbing, up the stairs to her bedroom.

Grabbing her duffel bag, she stuffed some clean socks and underwear on top of her books. She was leaving. Alex knew when she wasn't wanted.

chapter.11

Alex threw her duffel bag over her shoulder, forced herself to stop crying, and headed back downstairs. She hurried through the house and out the kitchen door. She heard Grandpa building something in the garage, so she hopped on her bike and headed across the backyard to a gravel alley that cut between the houses. If she avoided the front of the house, no one would know she'd disappeared till they called her to supper.

She arrived at Morgan's house fifteen minutes later. Until Alex pushed her wild hair back from her face and brushed her hand against her wet cheeks, she hadn't realized she was crying.

Morgan answered the door. "Hi! I didn't know—" Morgan peered close. "What's the matter?"

"You'll never believe this." Alex's words tumbled out in a rush as she told her best friend everything that had happened.

"I've always been there for my mom. But what happens when I need *her?* She ditches me!"

"What happened?" Morgan touched her arm. "Are you sure you didn't misunderstand her?"

"Yes, I'm sure. I have to get away for a couple days. Can I stay with you?"

Morgan paused. "You *sure* you want to run away?"

Not Morgan too! Alex turned to go. "If I can't stay here, I'll go somewhere else."

"Wait a minute. Come in." She stepped back and pulled Alex inside. "I have to tell Mom though."

Alex waited in the kitchen, her stomach rolling at the spicy smells coming from the oven. Morgan returned five minutes later with her mom.

"I just talked with your mother," Mrs. Cross said. "She agreed to you staying here a couple of days, but she said you're grounded here, the same as at home."

Alex wished she could leave, but realistically, where could she go? "I understand."

"She also said she wanted you to stay off the computer till tomorrow."

Alex clenched her jaws till they ached. She was caged even when she wasn't at home. And yet, what did it matter? She didn't want to tell Kevin she'd had another fight and run away from home. He'd never agree with what she'd done.

"I understand," she repeated.

"Don't worry, hon. It'll all work out." Mrs. Cross opened the oven door and checked the bubbling pasta. "Hope you're hungry. It's vegetarian lasagna tonight."

"With fat-free cheese," Morgan whispered, sticking a finger down her throat.

Alex smiled, but her heart—and stomach—just wasn't in it.

At lunch the next day at school, the TodaysGirls were already in a heated discussion when Alex and Morgan joined the table, where fashion magazines were strewn about.

"We don't have time for this," Bren said, waving her hands in the air.

"Time for what?" Morgan asked.

"To sew outfits for Sunday's Mother's Day Banquet. I mean, it's like Tuesday already!"

"Let's just buy matching outfits instead," Amber said.

Maya pointed her fork at Amber. "Exactly what I said."

Bren tapped her long nails on the table. "That's okay, except the style you chose won't look good on anyone but *you*. We don't all have your model's figure, Maya."

Jamie nodded. "I like the outfit Bren wants to get."

Maya snorted delicately. "You'll look like your legs were lopped off. You want long, not stubby."

Jamie laughed. "I wouldn't have long legs if you got me stilts."

"Hey girls," Morgan said, "what if we each choose our own style, but we get matching *colors* instead?"

Alex nodded. That sounded smarter to her. She could wear pants and a shirt even if Maya wore some skintight minidress.

Maya dabbed her lips with a napkin. "Not a bad idea from the infant. I could go for either red or fuschia."

Jamie shook her head. "Pastels, please. Baby blue maybe? Pink?"

"Gag," Alex said. "Black always works. Or army green."

"Good choice, Alex," Bren said. "We'll be the Mother's Day Marines."

"Well, I'm not wearing red or purple, I can tell you that." Alex stuffed a chicken pita in her mouth, letting half the lettuce dangle from her lips.

When the bell rang, Amber reminded them that Saturday night would be dress rehearsal at church.

Maya nodded. "Let's practice our song at the Gnosh Friday night too. We could use the karaoke player and run through it a few times before the crowd arrives."

Thank heavens, Alex thought, that she had the backup tape to practice with on her own. It still really burned her about being grounded from the Gnosh. Alex stood up and slung her bag over her shoulder. She had just turned to leave when Bren's words hit her like a hammer blow.

"Jamie, wait up," Bren said. "Did I tell you about my ride home with Kevin last night?"

Alex's heart stopped, then beat like a bass drum in her chest. She gripped the strap on her bag and couldn't move.

"No, what happened?" Jamie asked, gathering her notebook and pens.

"It was so cool," Bren gushed. "He knew the words to every song on the radio. Talk about a voice that makes you melt!"

Alex felt her arm start to quiver and loosened her grip on the strap. Head down, she strode out of the cafeteria, leaving Morgan behind. She couldn't believe it! Why had Kevin offered Bren a ride home? After singing with him in his garage, just the two of them?

Alex felt a stab of betrayal at the thought of Kevin singing to Bren while they rode in his car. Maybe Bren begged for a ride, she thought hopefully. Maybe it wasn't Kevin's idea at all. Still, Alex had seen Bren in action before. She knew how to get what she wanted.

Alex drifted through her afternoon classes in a fog. Her jumbled thoughts shifted back and forth between Kevin and her mom. The anger at her mom had worn off, but the pain of being left behind in Indiana was still raw. Alex had been so sure she was moving back home when school was out. How was she going to explain to her friends—and Kevin—that her own mom didn't want her back?

And yet, as the day wore on, Alex really regretted running off. Her mom would only be there five more days before flying home Monday after the banquet. She didn't really want to spend her mom's visit living at Morgan's. But how could she forgive her? It was asking too much. Even Alex couldn't pretend that *that* hadn't hurt.

She trudged home with Morgan after school, exhausted from having slept so little on the Crosses' couch the night before. Inside, Alex dropped her books in the hall. "Morgan, could I borrow your laptop for a while? I want to check my e-mail. And before you ask, I'm not grounded today."

"No problem. Better yet, use Maya's computer. She's shopping with Bren and won't be home for hours."

Alex cringed at the mention of Bren's name. "Thanks. I will."

In Maya's bedroom, Alex noted the closet full of clothes, the floor-length mirror, the fancy window treatments that matched the bedspread, and about twenty pairs of shoes lined up in the open closet. No wonder Maya was so full of herself.

When she logged on, there was just one e-mail message, a forward from her grandma.

Hi, honey. I know you're hurting, but I wish you'd come home. Things won't heal if you don't face them. Maybe you'll understand this little story that was sent to me by a friend. Love always, Grandma.

Curious, Alex clicked on the attachment icon and read:

Forgiving isn't pretending something doesn't hurt. Forgiving isn't being nice on the outside while you hold a grudge inside. Forgiveness has to start in your heart. Like a caterpillar in its cocoon, change has to come from the inside out. Most people settle for changing their outside actions, but pasting wings on a worm doesn't make a butterfly.

Alex slumped back in her chair, confused. Was her grandma calling her a fake? It sounded like acting nice didn't even count. Tears sprang to Alex's eyes. It wasn't fair. She'd tried so hard. She hadn't said *one* bad thing to her mom when she'd decided not to come for Mother's Day.

And she'd bit her tongue around Grandpa and acted as respectful as anybody could to that old toad. She'd even let Maya torture her with a makeover instead of telling her off. In her opinion, Alex had acted *real nice* to those people, and none of them had deserved it!

Even so, Grandma's story struck a nerve and reminded her of something. What was it? Alex frowned, staring through her tears at the blurry computer screen. Then she remembered.

Morgan had said something similar when they'd looked at the chrysalis in her backyard. She'd said that keeping her anger inside instead of forgiving could hurt her, like the butterfly Morgan had injured by "helping" it out of its cocoon. The struggle to break free from the cocoon made a butterfly's wings strong enough to fly. Morgan had said the struggle to forgive could make Alex stronger too.

Alex rubbed the knots in the back of her neck. Grandma was right that she still resented her mom (*and* Grandpa *and* Maya *and* Bren), but Alex was only human. She wiped her eyes on her shirttail and sniffled. She was doing the best she could. For some reason, though, it was never enough.

Alex decided to e-mail Kevin, telling him what had happened with her mom. She repeated Grandma's message about facing things so they could heal.

I can't face going home and being "nice" anymore! Do you understand?

She clicked *Send.*

As she rocked back and forth in Maya's swivel chair, a response from Kevin popped into her In box.

Hey there, Texas gal. I'm sorry you're dealing with so much right now. You've been bombarded! Your mom's decision must really hurt. Selfishly, I'm glad you'll be around this summer. Your grandmother's right about facing things so they'll heal. God will help you if you ask him. I wish I could help you too . . . I know. Let's go out and forget all our troubles. Kevin.

Man, I wish! Alex thought. She typed quickly.

You forget I'm grounded. Anyway, I can't date yet.

She clicked *Send*.
In just a minute she had another response.

I mean right here, right now. Online date. There's a great Teen Coffeehouse site. They have game rooms and a music room. Let's meet there.

Alex smiled for the first time in twenty-four hours.

Okay. I'm on Maya's big new computer and it should work.

Great! Go to www.teencoffeehouse.com and find the Arcade. I'll meet you there! Look for Gopher Bash.

Gopher Bash? Is that what you did on a cyberdate? In just thirty seconds, she'd found the site.

Welcome to the Teen Coffee House! Searching for a penpal or wanting to meet new friends? Teen Coffeehouse is the leading online community enabling secure connections between teens with similar interests or needs.

She registered as a "trial member," then entered the main room. It was set up like a coffeehouse with names on images leading to different rooms: Music Shops, Coming Events, Teen Poll, Live Music Videos, Homework Help, Advice Column, and an Arcade with online games.

Grinning, Alex clicked on Arcade, and a choice of games appeared: Asteroids, Ballistic Biscuit, Web War, Gopher Bash, Basketball. . . . She clicked on Gopher Bash and waited while a screen loaded. Twelve identical squares appeared, each with a gopher hole in the center. Across the bottom it read: Score 0, Level 1, Five tries. In a box at the right Player 1 was called KDMUSIC, and her own ITSTEXAS4ME was listed as Player 2.

In the next fifteen minutes, they played four games. When Alex clicked *Play*, a brown gopher with huge white eyes popped up erratically. Giggling, she bashed the gopher that popped out of the holes by clicking on him. He squealed like a pig and a goose egg popped up on his head. Her highest score was 190, which didn't come close to Kevin's 460.

After leaving the arcade, they entered Live Music Videos. There, Kevin introduced Alex to groups she'd never heard of like Newsboys, Out of Eden, and Sonic Flood. Alex loved watching the videos, knowing Kevin was watching the exact same thing at the exact same time. It was almost like a real date, or at least as real as Alex would ever have, if Grandpa had anything to say about it. Sighing, Alex wished for the hundredth time that her grandparents' antique computer could handle music and graphics like this.

From the music video room, they clicked over to the Music Shops where they could buy CD's, sheet music, and music software. Alex could understand Kevin's interest, but that room bored her stiff. After fifteen minutes in the Music Shop, they ducked into the Teen Espresso Chat. Kevin instant-messaged her in neon green ink while music pulsed in the background.

> KDMUSIC: This was fun! We'll have to do it again sometime. but right now I have to practice :*
>
> ITSTEXAS4ME: What's a :* ?
>
> KDMUSIC: You're sweet fourteen and never been cyberkissed?
>
> ITSTEXAS4ME: Cyberkissed?
>
> KDMUSIC: Hope you don't mind. Talk soon. Bye!

Alex's heart beat like a bongo drum. Grinning, she logged out of the Teen Coffeehouse, wondering how it'd feel to *really* be kissed.

Wednesday morning, Alex woke up early, confused until she remembered where she was—and why. Rolling over on the couch, she groaned at the ache in her back. She wasn't mad anymore, just deeply hurt. She'd never understand why her mom didn't want her to come home in June. Alex had always been good help to her mom, more a friend than a daughter. She never caused trouble or demanded anything. And what reward did she get? Nothing.

That night, Morgan set up her laptop in the kitchen for the TodaysGirls regular chat time. Maya always hogged the computer upstairs, even though it officially belonged to Maya, Morgan, and Jacob. Morgan hooked the laptop into the family's phone line in the kitchen but had to get off promptly at 8:30.

"Want to type?" Morgan asked as she logged on. "I can just watch tonight."

"No thanks. Actually, I need some clothes from home. Grandpa and Grandma have Wednesday night church, and hopefully Mom went with them. I want to run home, get my stuff, and get out before they come back."

"Okay. See you in a little while then."

Outside, Alex pedaled off through a lightly falling mist. She'd only gone a block when she remembered her empty duffel bag back in Morgan's kitchen. She needed it for her clothes. Making a U-turn, she hurried back to Morgan's. When she walked into the kitchen, Morgan was nowhere to be seen.

As Alex walked past the laptop, she saw the familiar magenta background of the TodaysGirls.com chat room. Leaning closer, she refreshed the screen and read. She had to reread the conversation twice before she could believe her own eyes.

chicChick: what about the outfits for the banquet, GFs? we MUST decide 2nite!

jellybean: i've gotta talk 2 u guys about a big problem.

there's something I have 2 tell Alex B4 she embar-
rasses herself @ the banquet

chicChick: where's Alex now?

jellybean: went home 2 get some clean clothes. She'll B
back soon.

nycbutterfly: clean clothes won't help her. I know she
doesn't have much $$, but that gal needs help. she
has -0- style!

chicChick: like get that girl 2 Glamour Shots!

jellybean: clothes isn't the main problem. I'll BRB, going
2 bathroom. Then I need ur advice.

chicChick: we aren't miracle workers, Morgan!

jellybean: we'd better B, or we're gonna look like fools
@ the banquet

Stunned, Alex backed away from the computer. They were all afraid she'd embarrass them at the banquet. What a bunch of back-stabbers! And they called themselves her friends!

Just then a toilet flushed and Morgan emerged from the half bath off the entryway. "Hi! That was fast." Morgan looked at Alex's face, then at the computer. "You didn't read—"

"Oh, yes I did! You're all stuck-up rich snobs. Even *you!* Well don't worry. I won't embarrass your precious little group with my tacky clothes at the banquet. I won't be there! My own mother doesn't want me, so why should I sing for her anyway?"

"Alex, wait!"

Throwing the duffel bag over her shoulder, Alex stormed out and biked home. The heavy mist had turned to drizzle, gathering on Alex's head and running down her face. She'd never felt so angry, or so betrayed, in her life. First her mom, now this! She wouldn't sing for that stupid banquet now, not even if they begged her.

When she arrived home, Grandpa's car was gone, and Alex gratefully entered the empty house. With any luck, she'd be in bed before anyone got home. She didn't want to talk to anyone, least of all her mother.

Alex flipped on the kitchen light. There on the table was a stack of pink printed programs for the Mother's Day Banquet. Alex found her name listed with her friends under "Banquet Entertainment." She was still staring at the programs when the phone rang.

Without thinking, she grabbed it. "Hello?"

"It's Morgan. Listen to me. You don't understand!"

Alex slammed the phone back down on its receiver. *Oh I understand plenty,* Alex thought grimly. And she hated every bit of it.

chapter.12

That night when her mom got home with Grandma and Grandpa, Alex was already in bed. She'd left a note taped to the closed bedroom door that merely said, "I'm back and asleep."

Her mom came into the bedroom but didn't turn on the lights. "Alex?" she whispered.

Alex breathed evenly. The last thing she could handle tonight was a talk with her mom.

"If you're awake," her mom said, "I need to say something to you." Her voice was barely a whisper, and Alex strained to hear while remaining perfectly still. "You've always been the best daughter, and you've done so much to help me. Now you have a normal life, with school and friends and no fighting parents." She paused again. "Leaving you in Edgewood a while longer is so hard for me, but it's my chance to do something good for *you* now."

She waited, then a moment later Alex heard her leave and close the door. The tears that had gathered in the corners of her eyes ran down the sides of her face.

Alex totally avoided her friends on Thursday and Friday, working in the computer lab instead of eating lunch. She ignored Morgan's e-mails and skipped the TodaysGirls chats. She didn't even tell Kevin what her "friends" had said behind her back. It was too humiliating. She simply said she'd moved back home, and he said he was "proud of her." *At least he likes* something *I did,* she thought.

Saturday night was dress rehearsal. If it weren't for Kevin playing backup and not wanting to disappoint Grandma, Alex wouldn't have shown up. It would take every last ounce of guts she had to pretend nothing was wrong.

At seven she biked over to the church. Alex could hear the band warming up before she opened the back door. Heading downstairs, Alex rolled her shoulders to loosen them up, took a deep breath, then strolled into the basement meeting room. Her friends were already grouped at the far end, and they fell silent when they saw her. Morgan smiled tentatively.

"Hey, Morgan!" Alex forced a grin as she tossed her hair back. "You ready for this?"

"I—I guess so. We should sound pretty good with the band."

Alex turned and waved at Kevin. "Yeah, we'll knock 'em dead tomorrow."

Jamie joined them then, followed by Amber. "We missed you online the last couple nights," Jamie said.

"I've been swamped!" Alex gave her prepracticed speech. "I got behind on my biology labs that were due yesterday. I'm spending the rest of my time with my mom before she leaves on Monday."

"Cool." Maya paused. "I, um, wondered if you were avoiding us because I was too hard on you about your clothes. I just wanted to help, but Morgan said I was mean. I'm really sorry."

"Well, maybe you were a little pushy, but I guess you were just trying to help."

"Exactly! Say, we decided on our color scheme. We're keeping it simple, just black skirts—long or short. Or black pants—long or capri. White tops, whatever kind you want."

Alex smiled and nodded, pretending to care. At least she had the black pants and white shirt. The shirt might even be clean.

Just then Maya clapped her hands sharply. "Listen up, everybody. Let's move along. I've got things to do and places to go."

The six girls lined up in front of the two microphone stands. Then Maya nodded at Kevin to start the introduction. Alex watched Maya and Bren sway to the beat, eyes closed, and she wanted to puke. Talk about phony Drama Queens.

Alex glanced over her shoulder. Kevin was looking right at her, and he winked. She'd been practicing their song with the tape, but this was so much better! At just the right time, she stepped up to the mike with Morgan and Jamie and sang out.

Is this one for the people?
Is this one for the Lord?
Or do I simply serenade for things I must afford?
You can jumble them together—

"Cut, cut!" Maya yelled. "Who's doing that?"

Amber laughed aloud. "Alex, was that you?"

"What a joker," Jamie agreed.

Bren stood with her hands on her hips. "We don't have time to fool around."

"I couldn't sing that off-key if I tried!" Maya nodded at Kevin. "Start over. And no more gags, girls. I don't have all night."

Jamie patted Alex's shoulder. "You crack me up!"

Alex felt like she'd been punched with boxing gloves from five different directions. "Real funny. I bet I practiced more than any of *you*."

"You mean you weren't trying to be funny?" Bren demanded.

Total silence fell abruptly, as if someone had pressed a Mute button.

Maya finally broke the awkward stillness. "Morgan, is *this* what you were trying to warn us about?"

Alex held her breath, looking down the line of her friends. Each girl quickly looked away. Reality slowly sank in. They all thought Alex sounded horrible! But why? What was wrong with her voice? She glanced at Morgan, but her best friend was staring at the floor. Did Morgan think her singing stunk too?

It didn't make sense! Why would they wait till now to tell her she sang off-key? They'd heard her sing plenty of times before. Or . . . had they really?

With a sinking feeling, each Karaoke Night flashed briefly through Alex's mind. The first time she'd barely sung because she didn't know the words. Morgan *had* looked startled once when Alex sang in her ear. Was it because she was so awful? The next Karaoke Night Morgan had tried to stop her parents from dragging Alex up front to sing again. Had that been why? That night, Coach's boy had grabbed the mike after insulting her singing, then drowned Alex out. Actually, no one but Morgan had really heard her or knew her voice was off-key.

Alex's eyes opened wide as the truth dawned on her. Was *that* what Morgan had started to tell the others in the chat room the other night? When Alex blew up after reading Morgan's message, Morgan had apparently changed her mind about telling.

Alex was aghast when tears filled her eyes. Her friends had believed she was playing a prank, but she'd really sung the best she knew how. She felt so humiliated. No one said a word. As if in a trance, Alex walked out of the meeting room and upstairs. Outside she stumbled to the bike rack, then heard footsteps on the gravel behind her.

"Wait!" Kevin said, catching up to her. "I know their laughing hurt. I'm really sorry."

Alex wiped her eyes with her sleeve. "You don't sound very surprised at their reaction though."

Kevin shuffled one foot back and forth. "Please don't take this personally, but I knew the first time you sang in my garage that you were tone deaf."

"Thanks a lot!"

"It's not a put-down. Honest. Singing just isn't your gift. We all have different talents."

Alex stared at the ground. Music was Kevin's life. How could he ever be interested in a girl who literally got laughed out of her singing group?

"I'm sorry I didn't tell you before. I didn't want to hurt your feelings."

"Like I don't hurt even worse *now?*" She hopped on her bike.

"Don't run off like last time. Talk to me."

Alex stood, shoulders rigid. How could she put it into words: her mom's betrayal, Grandpa's meanness, her friends' constant criticism. A person could only take so much. If she was such a loser that her own mom didn't want her around, how long would it take Kevin to realize she wasn't worth *his* time either?

Without another word, Alex pedaled away from the church, down a dark street toward home. The hurt and embarrassment brought tears to her eyes, and snatches of the song pulsed through her mind in rhythm with her pedaling: "What if I stumble, what if I fall? What if I lose my step and I make fools of us all?"

Alex faked being sick the next morning to skip church. "You just rest," her mom said. "You want to be able to sing for the banquet tonight."

Oh sure, Alex thought, *I'd have everyone rolling on the floor laughing.* Aloud she just said, "Happy Mother's Day." She could barely look at her mom though. She was flying back to Texas the next day, and she hadn't said a thing about Alex even coming home to visit during the summer. *Fine,* Alex thought as her mom left for church, *I don't need you either. I don't need anybody.*

At six o'clock that night she was still lying in bed when her mom and grandma came in, dressed now in spring skirts and lacy blouses, ready to leave for the banquet.

Grandma patted Alex's knee under the comforter. "I'm so sorry you got that nasty flu bug that's going around. We'll miss you tonight."

Her mom studied her quizzically but said nothing. She just hugged Alex and pushed her hair back off her face. Alex turned her face to the wall.

After Alex heard their car drive away, she padded downstairs to make a sandwich but paused at the bottom of the steps. Grandpa was in his recliner, staring sadly at something in his lap. Alex stood on tiptoe to see better.

Balanced on Grandpa's knees were two framed photos. Alex

recognized them from the top of the bookcase. One was a first-grade picture of her mother. The other was a photograph of Alex at the same age. Compared to how different they looked now, she and her mother had borne a remarkable resemblance as little girls.

What was going on? Was Grandpa remembering how harsh he'd been with her mother when he drove her away? Alex wondered. According to Grandma, he had never learned to bend or say he was wrong about anything. It had cost him a close relationship with his only daughter. Was he afraid he'd made the same mistake with Alex?

Quietly Alex backed up the stairs. Grandma often joked that Alex was stubborn like Grandpa, "a chip off the old block." *Was* she? How she hated the idea! But what if it were true? Was she going to hang on to her hurt and resentment, and lose out on the last night of her mom's visit because of it?

Alex didn't have to think very long. She ached for things to be right with her mom. In her room, she quickly dressed. She buttoned the nicest white shirt she had and pulled on a pair of black jeans. "I'm better," she said to Grandpa as she flew through the living room a minute later. "I'll be at the banquet."

Outside, she climbed on her bike and headed to the church. She might miss the meal, but the entertainment was afterward. Only how could she face everyone? Deep down she knew Morgan had tried to protect her from embarrassment. And Maya, in her own pushy way, was just trying to help her social life. And Bren really couldn't be blamed for her interest in Kevin. She had no idea that Alex had feelings for him—only Morgan knew about them e-mailing and cyberdating. Kevin had tried to protect her feelings, too, and even her mom thought she was giving Alex a better life by leaving her in Edgewood for now.

But when she arrived at the church and saw the full parking lot, she shivered in spite of the warm evening. What was she doing there? She still couldn't sing! She was so tempted to turn around and go home. It took all her courage to enter the church and walk down the stairs to the meeting room. Women's murmuring voices and laughter blended with the clinking of silverware. Alex hung back and peered around the doorway. Her friends were eating at the far table, and Kevin was arranging the music for the band.

Just then he turned and caught a glimpse of her. He hurried over. "I hoped you'd come." Kevin's voice was quiet. "You're just in time to sing."

"I don't think I can. I shouldn't be here." Alex stared at the floor. "I feel like such a jerk. Riding over here, I finally understood some things. I know you and Morgan were just trying to protect my feelings by not saying anything." She leaned against the stair railing. "I've barely spoken to my mom. She doesn't want me to come home after all, but I know she just wants me to have a better life here. Even Grandpa wants to help me not make the same mistakes Mom did. I don't know what's wrong with me—"

"Stop, Alex. You're not a jerk." Kevin covered one of her

hands with his own. "You have to forgive *yourself* before you can forgive others."

Alex wished he'd never move his hand. "How do you always say just the right thing?"

"Ah, I'm just older and wiser, that's all." Kevin grinned. At that moment Alex's grandmother approached the microphone. "Come on," Kevin said. "Show time."

"Ladies, ladies!" Grandma waited till the chattering died down. "After this delicious meal, it's my pleasure to introduce our entertainment tonight. Before I do, I want you to meet a very special guest, my daughter, Gail Diaz." Grandma beamed and motioned for Alex's mom to join her up front. Polite applause broke out as she made her way to the microphone. "Gail's home from Texas this week for Mother's Day, and that makes it a wonderful day indeed for me."

Grandma kissed Alex's mom on the cheek, and even from the doorway Alex saw the tenderness in her mom's eyes. Their closeness tugged at Alex's heart. The last of her resentment melted away in the warmth of their love. Maybe, if she stepped forward now to sing, it would make the night special for her own mother too.

And yet . . . How *could* she? Unless she lip-synced, her tone-deaf singing would ruin the song and this perfect moment.

Grandma stood with her arm around her daughter. "As mothers, we all fear making mistakes with our children. But sometimes those very struggles, with God's help, can produce a child's greatest strength." Grandma turned to the band and smiled, then motioned for the girls to come up. "They'll be singing about this in a beautiful song called 'What If I Stumble?'"

Kevin grabbed Alex's hand. "That's our cue."

Eyes down, Alex followed Kevin to the front of the large meeting room. After walking out last night, she couldn't make herself look at her friends. They must be horrified that she was going to sing. She moved toward the mike, but Kevin kept hold of her hand. "Can you take Shonn's part? He got sick and couldn't come."

"Me? On the bass?"

"Sure. You learned the chords, remember?" Suddenly it dawned on her what Kevin was doing.

"But—but—" Alex protested.

Kevin led her back to stand beside him and handed her Shonn's guitar. "You know the music. Just follow me."

Aware of her friends' curious stares, Alex slipped the shoulder strap over her head. Standing in a row just in front of her, dressed in black and white, were the TodaysGirls. Her mom and Grandma sat beaming in front-row seats. Alex smiled sheepishly.

Kevin waited for Maya's signal, then played the introduction. Nick joined on the drums, and Graham at the keyboard. Then at Kevin's nod, Alex added the simple bass chords. They repeated in easy patterns, but she kept her eyes glued to Kevin's hands.

'Cause I see the trust in their eyes
Though the sky is falling
They need your love in their lives
Compromise is calling

As she listened to the words, they stirred her as nothing had in a long time. Her own sky was falling; her mom was flying home the next day and leaving Alex behind again. How could she trust her mom—or her friends—again? She glanced up to find Kevin singing right to her.

You see, God's love for us
Is so much greater than our mistakes
He loves us as we are, and not as we should be
He wants to take you, he wants you to come as you are.
What if I stumble, what if I fall?
What if I lose my step and I make fools of us all?
Will the love continue
When my walk becomes a crawl?
What if I stumble, and what if I fall?

When the last chorus ended, Alex finally looked up and met her mother's eyes. In the words of the song, she desperately wanted to ask her mother the same questions. Did her mom understand the fear that lived in Alex and the rate at which it grew? Did their family struggles really have a purpose? Even more, did her mother really love her? Alex slipped the strap over her head and handed the bass to Kevin, knowing she was much too afraid to ever really ask those questions.

Turning, she caught Morgan's eye and couldn't mistake the warmth and caring she saw there. Amber smiled, and Maya gave her a thumbs-up sign. Jamie squeezed her arm. "Way to go," she whispered.

After the applause died down, her friends returned to their table and Alex went to join her mom. However, her mother stood and moved forward to where Kevin waited at the microphone.

"What's going on?" Alex whispered to her grandma as she took her mom's chair.

"I have no idea!"

Kevin cleared his throat. "As you all know, Gail Diaz is here from Texas to visit her mother and her daughter. As a special surprise for them, she has prepared a song of her own called 'A Mother's Heart.'" He handed Alex's mom the mike, then moved back to his own music. Nodding at Nick and Graham, they began the long, slow introduction.

Alex glanced at Grandma, who stared straight ahead, her hand at her throat. Alex could barely breathe either. She couldn't believe it! How had they worked that out? When? Then she recalled the previous Sunday when she'd seen her mom give Kevin a large envelope. That must have been sheet music!

Alex's eyes never left her mother's face as she sang about "beautiful hearts with limitless love" and "pure hearts seeing goodness in others." Alex had almost forgotten what a great voice her mom had. If only she had inherited some of it herself!

Her mom paused while the band played a quiet background interlude. Then she looked at both Alex and Grandma and sang the last verse.

A mother's heart is a generous heart
That knows the true meaning of giving,
In trying to love the people around her
By setting them free—and forgiving.

As Alex listened to the words, she realized life wasn't easy for her mom, and it hadn't been easy for Grandma either. They had both done the best they could, and part of loving each other was forgiving. It was time. It was long past time.

When the song ended, Alex glanced around. There wasn't a dry eye in the house. Her mom put the microphone back on the stand, smiled her thanks at Kevin, then walked toward Alex and Grandma. Alex stood, hardly able to breathe. Without a word needing to be said, she reached out and clung to her mother. Alex might never totally understand her mom's reasons for doing things, but she'd never doubt her love again.

Alex's mom's flight home Monday morning was scheduled for 6:30, so it was a yawning Alex who waited with her grandparents while her mom got her seat assignment.

"All done," her mom said a moment later. "Window seats all the way." She set down her carry-on luggage, then hugged Alex close. "Oh, how I wish you could come home with me now."

"Me, too, Mom. Tell Dad I'll visit this summer."

"I will. I can't wait."

Just then a noisy group arrived in the waiting area, and Alex whirled around at the sound of familiar voices. "I don't believe it!" Morgan, Maya, Bren, Jamie, and Amber waved and grinned. "What are you guys doing here?"

Maya handed Alex's mom a bouquet of daffodils. "We couldn't let a TodaysGirl mom leave without a proper good-bye."

"That's right," Bren said, turning to Alex. "We were like *shocked* that you had such a cool mom. She rocks!"

Grinning, Alex placed one hand behind her frizzy head and the other on her hip. "You should have known by looking at me."

The intercom crackled to life, and a voice said, "Now boarding the 6:25 flight to Dallas. Passengers in rows 22 to 30 will board first."

"Guess that's me." Alex's mom sniffed the daffodils. "Thanks, girls. It was a pleasure meeting you." Next she hugged her mother. "I'm so grateful for your making this trip possible."

"I just wish you could have stayed longer."

Alex's mom turned toward her dad, but she hesitated. Grandpa rubbed a hand across his face, then stepped forward and gave her an awkward hug. "Take care of yourself."

"I will, Dad."

Finally Gail Diaz turned toward her daughter. Time stood still, and Alex felt her mouth start to quiver. Then, without caring who watched, she wrapped her arms tightly around her mom. She squeezed her eyes shut, but it didn't stop them from filling with tears. They clung to each other until final boarding was announced.

Then her mom gave Alex an extra hard squeeze, sniffled, and pulled back. She gently touched Alex's cheek. "Don't ever doubt how much I love you."

Alex felt like her heart was about to burst. "I won't."

Turning back to Grandpa, Alex's mom said, "Thanks for taking care of my little girl." She paused. "Just let her spread her wings sometimes."

"I will do my best," he said, clearing his throat, "but absolutely no dating till she's sixteen."

Alex glanced at her mom and rolled her eyes, but she didn't argue. Actually, Grandpa's rule didn't sound so bad. Cyberdating— and cybersmooching—was all she could handle for now.

Net Ready, Set, Go!

I hope my words and thoughts please you.
Psalm 19:14

The characters of TodaysGirls.com chat online in the safest—and maybe most fun—of all chat rooms! They've created their own private Web site and room! Many Christian teen sites allow you to create your own private chat rooms, and there are other safe options.

Work with your parents to develop a list of safe, appropriate chat rooms. Earn Internet freedom by showing them you can make the right choices. *Honor your father and your mother (Deuteronomy 5:16).*

Before entering a chat room, you'll select a user name. Although you can use your real name, a nickname is safer. Most people choose one that says something about who they are, like Amber's name, faithful1. Don't be discouraged if the name you select is already taken. You can use a similar one by adding a number at its end.

No one will notice your grammar in a chat room. Don't worry if you spell something wrong or forget to capitalize. Some people even misspell words on purpose. You might see a sentence like How R U?

But sometimes it's important to be accurate. Web site and e-mail addresses must be exact. Pay close attention to whether letters are upper- or lowercase. Remember that Web site addresses don't use some punctuation marks, such as hyphens and apostrophes. (That's why the "Today's" in TodaysGirls.com has no apostrophe!) And instead of spaces between words, underlines are often used to_make_a_space. And sometimes words just run together like onebigword.

When you're in a chat room, remember real people are typing the words that appear on your screen. Treat them with the same respect you expect from them. Don't say anything you wouldn't want repeated in Sunday school. *Do for other people what you want them to do for you (Luke 6:31).*

Sometimes people say mean, hurtful things—things that make us angry. This can happen in chat rooms, too. In some chat rooms, you can highlight a rude person's name and click a button that says, "ignore," which will make his or her comments disappear from your screen. You always have the option to switch rooms or sign off. If a particular person becomes a continual problem, or if someone says something especially vicious, you should report this problem user to the chat service. *Ask God to bless those who say bad things to you. Pray for those who are cruel (Luke 6:28–29).*

Remember that Internet information is not always factual. Whether you're chatting or surfing Web sites, be skeptical about information and people. Not everything on the Internet is true. You don't have to be afraid of the Internet, but you should always be cautious. Practice caution with others even in Christian chat rooms.

It's OK to chat about your likes and dislikes, but *never* give out personal information. Do not tell anyone your name, phone number, address, or even the name of your school, team, church, or neighborhood. Be cautious. . . . *You will be like sheep among wolves. So be as smart as snakes. But also be like doves and do nothing wrong. Be careful of people (Matthew 10:16–17).*

N 2 DEEP & STRANGER ONLINE

16/junior
e-name: faithful1
best friend: Maya
site area: Thought for the Day

Confident. Caring. Swimmer. Single-handedly built
TodaysGirls.com Web site. Loves her folks.
Big brother Ryan drives her nuts! Great friend.
Got a problem? Go to Amber.

AMBER
THOMAS

JAMIE CHANDLER

PLEASE REPLY! & PORTRAIT OF LIES

15/sophomore
e-name: rembrandt
best friend: Bren
site area: Artist's Corner

Quiet. Talented artist. Works at the Gnosh Pit
after school. Dad left when she was little.
Helps her mom with younger sisters Jordan and
Jessica. Baby-sits for Coach Short's kids.

ALEX DIAZ

4GIVE&4GET & TANGLED WEB

14/freshman
e-name: TX2step
best friend: Morgan
site area: Entertain Us

Spicy. Hot-tempered Texan. Lives with grandparents because
of parents' problems. Won state in freestyle swimming at her
old school. Snoops. Into everything. Breaks the rules.

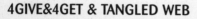

POWER DRIVE & R U 4 REAL?
16/junior
e-name: nycbutterfly
best friend: Amber
site area: What's Hot—What's Not

MAYA CROSS

Fashion freak. Health nut. Grew up in New York City.
Small town drives her crazy. Loves to dance.
Dad owns the Gnosh Pit. Little sis Morgan is also
a TodaysGirl.

BREN MICKLER

UNPREDICTABLE & LUV@FIRST SITE
15/sophomore
e-name: chicChick
best friend: Jamie
site area: Smashin' Fashion

Funny. Popular. Outgoing. Spaz. Cheerleader. Always late.
Only child. Wealthy family. Bren is chatting—
about anything, online and off, except when
she's eating junk food.

FUN E-FARM & CHAT FREAK
14/freshman
e-name: jellybean
best friend: Alex
site area: Feeling All Write

MORGAN
CROSS

The Web-ster. Spends too much time online. Overalls.
M&M's. Swim team. Tries to save the world. Close to her
family—when her big sister isn't bossing her around.

Cyber Glossary

Bounced mail An e-mail that has been returned to its sender.

Chat A live conversation—typed or spoken through microphones—among individuals in a chat room.

Chat room A "place" on the Internet where individuals meet to "talk" with one another.

Crack To break a security code.

Download To receive information from a more powerful computer.

E-mail Electronic mail sent through the Internet.

E-mail address An Internet address where e-mail is received.

File Any document or image stored on a computer.

Floppy disk A small, thin plastic object that stores information to be accessed by a computer.

Hacker Someone who tries to gain unauthorized access to another computer or network of computers.

Header Text at the beginning of an e-mail that identifies the sender, subject matter, and the time at which it was sent.

Home page A Web site's first page.

Internet A worldwide electronic network that connects computers to each other.

Link Highlighted text or a graphic element that may be clicked with the mouse in order to "surf" to another Web site or page.

Log on/Log in To connect to a computer network.

Modem A device that enables computers to exchange information.

The Net The Internet.

Newbie A person who is learning or participating in something new.

Online To have Internet access. Can also mean to use the Internet.

Surf To move from page to page through links on the Web.

Upload To send information to a more powerful computer.

The Web The World Wide Web or WWW.